To L

There have been many theories that Jack the Ripper might have been a woman. The theories have been tested throughout time and still there is no clear evidence as to the identity of the Whitechapel murderer!

They never found Jack so perhaps it was Jane

The murder victims are real but the story is fictional, the manner in which they met their sorry end has still to be discovered. A murderous tale of sordid death set deep in the misty shadows of the thick London fog.

Caution
Contains Graphic content

May the unfortunate women who lost their lives to Jack the Ripper, rest in eternal peace. Their vengeance is forever lost in history and time.

<u>RIP</u>

Elizabeth

Martha

Mary

Annie

Liz

Catherine

Mary

*****

The names of the ripper victims are accurate; however, the body of the story is purely fictional.

The tale is told through the eyes of Jane, a twenty four year old, deranged young widow and bereaved mother of stillborn twins. She has no concept of reality. Her only quest is to appease her pain

Disclaimer

No disrespect is intended and any inference to the personalities or morals of the deceased, is purely fictional and coincidental and is only for the purpose of the storyline.

Perhaps it was Jane

By Irene Husk

A twist on the mystery of Jack the Ripper

***

Put vague and futile thoughts of Jack the Ripper out of question as who knows, perhaps it was Jane

With heartfelt condolences to the women and the families affected by the heinous crimes of Jack the Ripper

Chapter 1

Elizabeth

Chapter 1

Elizabeth

It had been a very uneventful April night during the spring-time of 1888. The thick London fog masked a multitude of sins. Prostitutes argued for a fair price, as loud drunken brawls created black eyes and split lips. The streets of Whitechapel held to ransom, those trapped in an unfortunate existence of poverty.

I studied two policemen as they stood at the corner of Wentworth Street. The silver badges on their peaked helmets glinted, with each flicker of the light from the gas lamps above their heads and their partly concealed notebooks, pencils and whistles created an obvious outline in their tunic pockets. The hefty truncheons that hung from their leather belts were insignificant to me, as I was not about to reveal my act.

The officers were ready to change shift, it was almost midnight and the men were tired after a busy evening suppressing the petty, opportunistic theft on the streets. I knew I had only half an hour before their replacements arrived and I checked under my shawl, to ensure my wrap of trusted tools would be easily accessible.

The officers shook hands and I knew it was time; I scanned the street ahead and caught sight of an intoxicated Miss Smith, as she stumbled, ungainly from the tavern; her grubby cotton skirt hardly reached her ankles, she wore a tight bodice, her bare shoulders and her neck were emphasized by her barely concealed, ample bosoms and a woollen shawl hung loosely around her shoulders. I had timed it perfectly.

My eyes followed the odd listed gait of the first officer, as he disappeared into the heavy mist, followed quickly by the other, taller one. I knew he would pass back that way on his journey home for the night. I had often seen him around Whitechapel, as I had carefully studied the local officers as they strode purposefully along on their regular beat. I had spent several weeks, discreetly watching them, it was crucial to make it my business, as I had to know every movement of the constables, it was imperative to my work. A plan well laid could easily be thwarted by an oversight.

During the time spent becoming familiar with these men, I had learned their usual routines and I recognized their individual quirks. I realised I would have to perform my act quickly. The taller officer was my only concern, as he lived fairly close to my chosen workplace for the night. I was sure I would manage to complete my job before he returned, as I could perceive his shadow and distinguish the sound of his boots on the cobbles, therefore I was fairly confident that I would remain unnoticed.

Yes! I could easily identify his approach should I need to make haste, I was certain of this. He was distinctly tall, he walked slightly bent forward from his thin hips, always with both hands behind his back and his stride was wide and quick. In the yellow light of the gas lanterns his shadow became elongated.

I drew my gaze to Elizabeth Smith, the filthy whore had spread her infections for the very last time and tonight was her turn to die: I ambled close behind her, as she made her way towards Osbourne Street. I waited for the three men that had been harassing her, to pass on the other side of the street, then checked it was clear before quickly inserting the knife into her ear; she fell to the floor and I turned her body so that she lay on her back. It was easier to take the trophies that way. I fumbled in the darkness, it was not easy and time was getting along. I tried to continue but luck was not on my side. My tools dropped to the floor and I had to feel around for them in the dark, it was difficult and I became frustrated as I searched blindly for them.

Her stomach was tough, like cow hide and I was forced to hew the ear from her head as it caught on my button. Time was still my enemy and I was compelled to stop, as I heard footsteps approaching. I failed to complete the task in its entirety and it had peeved me greatly. Instead, I quickly beat about her face until she became almost unrecognizable, before forcing a discarded milk bottle into her disgustingly noxious vagina. I stood over her for a short while until the footsteps became closer and I slipped my leather wrap inside my shawl and walked on. I smiled at the tall officer and he smiled back!

I slipped through the streets, past aproned landlords throwing out vagabonds, down the dimly lit alleys packed with prostitutes and along the terraces filled with scuttling rats and thick smog.

Sinister figures in dark capes and top hats, sidestepped the many flaming hot braziers that were surrounded by raucous men, idly smoking and slapping backs, ignorant of the tedium and hardship engulfing them. I pulled the folds of my shawl around me and disappeared through the gates of the park. It was shrouded in darkness and the only sounds to be witnessed; were that of grunting customers as they went about their loathsome gratification, the results of which could be so randomly cast away from the wombs of the desperate women.

I hurried along in my own private misery and crept through the ornate gates, into the rear of the house and through the servant's entrance, unseen and unheard. I climbed the wide stairs to the sanctity of my room and there, I hid the simple dress and shawl in a big cloth sack. I put it in a box underneath my bed and I washed the stickiness from me.

I carefully hid the soft leather wrap with the sharp tools inside it, at the bottom of my wardrobe, then I climbed into my soft bed. My first task had not gone as well as I had hoped, but I had learned a very good lesson.

I would be more prepared for the next time. There would be no hesitation, alas my mental fortitude had slipped a little, in the face of adversity, and the fear of being caught had undermined my skills. I had almost failed to close the eyes of Miss Elizabeth for good and I did not dare to consider the alternative. My mission was bound to succeed but only if I were to rid the streets of the scourge that inhabits them, without chastity or grace and I must continue without exposure. The adrenaline rush had enhanced my mood and I could not sleep, I lay in quiet contemplation until the dawn gently broke.

I checked the newspapers daily but there was nothing about Elizabeth. There was no point in wasting my time unless they were going to die; I was sure I had done a good enough job and I scanned the pages for many days, until I eventually learned that death from her injuries, had at last befallen her.

The press said it was a gang of men but it was by my hands, mine alone, I did it and I rejoiced in my success. So foul a woman suffered so foul a death and the blame idly apportioned to another. It had been rather an inauspicious start to my good cause, however, the police were blindly unaware that much worse was yet to come and I was liberated.

I would do whatever was required of me, to rid society of the wanton epidemic of disease spreading whores. Vile creatures of the night unclean debauched and free of basic morality. The cause of my pain, a burning and everlasting pain, that of the nature that required healing by atonement: There would be no alternative conclusion, as I would not allow it.

The unspeakable abomination, so immoral and tawdry a devilish contamination, that infiltrated and soiled every recess of the community. In my mind's eye, it appeared somewhat like a recurring pustule on the streets. It was a carbuncle to be lanced.

Greater care would have to be taken, I had narrowly missed detection, it would surely have thwarted my intention, should I have been caught on my first endeavour and the need to check my timings, was paramount.

Indeed, time was of the utmost essence, if I were to continue well with my quest and complete my tasks in their entirety. The recent near miss had caused me to realise that there was no room for blunders, if I were to forge my plan to use the cover of the night as my camouflage. I would have to make haste, as to carve through flesh takes time and the blood-flow inhibits the location of the trophies.

There was a lot to be learned and it would be a simple case of trial and error but the grey fog and the dark were my friends and they would aid me greatly. My hands were bruised from the effort of my night's work but I was enveloped in a most peculiar satisfaction.

It had been a clumsy first attempt and it was purely by the grace of God himself, that the mission had been completed and Elizabeth was now dead. The newspapers warn to beware of the streets at night as there are vagabonds and men with knives, they tell of brutality and fear and they tell of poor Elizabeth. The newspapers set the blame on three men who attacked her so viciously then left her to die on the street; but it was not so, as these men had simply passed on their way. The hospital failed to save Elizabeth and she died of her injuries

Whoever would have imagined, that fate itself would intervene and finish the job for me!

Chapter 2

Martha

Chapter 2

Martha

Another bank holiday, August is a good time to die! A multitude of merry-makers filled the streets, I saw two young soldiers hanging around the corner of Whitechapel Road, I knew what they were looking for and I pitied their souls.

I had not bargained for that pearly girl to be hanging around with Martha. My best laid plans had been compromised and the dilemma only served to exasperate me. Luckily, as they agreed their prices, they separated and Martha linked her arm in that of the young soldier with the fair hair and moustache and they walked towards the arch into George Yard. It was a good place, it was dark and quiet there, so I was confident that I could work undetected, I waited until they had finished their four-penny knee tremble and the soldier went on his way, perhaps to continue drinking at the seedy tavern. Martha bent down to straighten her dark green cotton skirt over her bland brown petticoat; she patted her hair and donned her black bonnet, then made her way towards the light emanating from the imposing stone archway; and so did I.

She failed to see me as I stood before her; I already held aloft Arthur's ceremonial bayonet in one hand and the long handled knife in the other. I swung both blades in a frenzied display of inner strength. I could feel the warm blood as it splashed on to my face and although I could not see too well, I knew I had hit my target, as I felt the spray from her jugular drench me.

The surge of pleasure, as the blade of the knife hit bone resounded on me and I let out a cry of triumph. It was done; all that was required was to remove those organs that represented her life. One necessary little act, the final one, one that would dehumanise the insignificant and loathsome creature, now lying defunct at my feet.

I dragged her lifeless body to the stairwell and turned her carcass on to its' back. It was totally impossible to see the prizes, her bodice was very tight and there were too many buttons. Her skirt and petticoats were cumbersome and I struggled hard to maintain my balance on the narrow steps. My arms ached from the weight of her body and I slipped on the spilled blood.

The impenetrable darkness was my cover however, it was difficult to work and I had to use my sense of touch to locate the area of the trophies. It was to be yet another disappointing outcome, as I had failed to consider the effect that the inability to see, would have on the result. I lingered for a moment then hid the knives in the soft leather wrap and carefully tucked it inside the bustle of my skirt.

The deed had been done and although I had not fully completed the task in hand, it was good practice for the remainder of the quest. I needed to hone my skills and find a way to draw my tools more easily.

It was food for thought and it filled me with a determination to find the solution. I smiled inwardly in the knowledge that at least the world was now free of two of its offensive monsters.

It was such a good feeling, as I imagined Martha in her grubby and semen stained drawers, lying abandoned and void of life, on the filthy pavement. Not so pretty now my dear.

Martha had not cried out, no disturbance had been heard by the residents, tucked up and fast asleep and all within a few yards from us; the passing cab driver, late home from his shift, dismissed her lifeless body as a homeless drunk and he had almost tripped over her, but had managed to step aside the extinct whore and retire to his bed for the night.

I picked through the grime of the street, being careful not to bring attention to myself. The kerbside was littered with drunks and unfortunates who had nowhere else to go. A rat scuttled by and began nibbling at a discarded piece of crust and a starving dog lay shaking as it was kicked out of the way by passers by

An unattended child sat in his own filth, in a big dirty pram, as his mother copulated in loud abandonment against the nearby wall. Men urinated in the streets and the prostitutes shamelessly offered their ugly wares. The haggard old woman selling a box or two of matches, glared at me as I passed by without making a purchase. The pungent stench of the stale London air filled my lungs and it was a struggle not to vomit, as I crept silently along the littered alleyways of the teeming slums. The fog shrouded my presence, I was truly a ghost.

Martha was void of life, of that I was sure. My hands had become sticky with the congealing blood, as the cold air dried it to my skin and clothes. I hastily made my way, homewards, it was too dangerous on the streets at night and I did not want to get embroiled in anything I could not easily control, and not only that, I had the greatest desire to cleanse away the foul contamination from my being. I was just a little more confident, as I knew I would do better next time.

Unfortunately, this time, I had again failed to collect my trophies and I was slightly dismayed, however, it was only natural, that as a beginner I would make mistakes, after all, making mistakes is how we learn our trade and we all have to start somewhere.

My leather wrap was difficult to discern in the darkness and I had almost dropped it in my haste to get away. I would have to find another way in which to conceal and carry my tools, I required them to be more quickly accessible to me. The bayonet had been rendered useless, as it had snapped on impact as it hit bone, but no matter, as other tools abounded in the big metal cabinet in Arthur's study. There would be many more to choose from; many that would be shorter and made, perhaps, of stronger steel.

The young soldiers were long gone, but, I knew they would become suspects. Leave our soldiers alone, if you please, as they will squabble enough between themselves. They are not for taking the lives of any other, than those who threaten our queen; as what perfect savage, would dare inflict such wounds on a defenceless woman.

The newspapers say there is a perplexing character that leaves very little evidence or clues and they say the perpetrator is a madman. The safety of the townsfolk has been put to question and the people are afraid. The witnesses will be unclear, as the victims are women of the night and the customers would be many and elusive. A frightful concern was born in the squalor of the crime consumed streets of Whitechapel in 1888. I however, was not afraid.

I read the front page with utter contempt, there should be no place in society for the female beasts and how very dare they say I have a sociopathic mind. I possess one more wilful and committed to my cause, than any lesser being would comprehend. I folded the paper and left it on the table, as I had no inclination to read lies.

My determination and resolve outweighs the risks of getting caught. I don't want to get caught, not yet, not until my work is done. There are still a few souls to send to the devil and they would be gone by my hand. I stood assured of that.

Chapter 3

Whitechapel

Chapter 3

Whitechapel

Despite our privileged life, in the midst of the significant wealth of the suburbs; our house was just a stones-throw from the district of Whitechapel, a place renowned for its lawlessness, a most sordid deprived and desolate place and one of the poorest areas of London town. A destitute place where the residents live in abject poverty; and rampant crime abounds. There were some traders making a living and running fairly successful businesses along the bigger roads like Commercial Street, but for the greatest number of the impoverished society, a life of hardship was endured.

It was fair to say that there were a few respected areas scattered amongst the dirty cobbled streets in the smoggy East End, however, for the main part it had its slums and a number of no go areas where even the police were too afraid to venture. The busy railways caused blinding pollution as the imposing engines thundered past the maze of tiny and cramped terraced houses that spilled thick black soot from the coal fed chimneys. A dirty blackness mingled with the caustic fumes from the factories and caused an unpleasant, gritty mist that filled the air.

The standard of housing was extremely poor; the sanitation was non-existent and raw sewage ran through the overpopulated streets. The poor visibility was a natural curtain for criminal activities and violence and the smoke emitting from the liberally used coal and gas, caused diseases of the chest that consumed the population forced to bear the hardship of life there.

The men worked on the railways or in the factories, some laboured at the docks, they were mostly employed on a random day to day basis and their jobs had no security. There was very little work for women and many of them ended up in the workhouse, or were forced into prostitution simply to survive and to eat. Many women became alcoholic, as drink was their only escape from the horrors of their daily life. There were numerous lodging or doss houses where the homeless or destitute could find a place to sleep, but they overflowed and offered unhygienic sheets and rat infested rooms. The landlords of the taverns and inns appeared to be the only ones profiting from the poverty and depression that was so apparent there.

There was a fairly large Jewish population and they lived in their own communities, they were unpopular due to their business acumen as they often made great success out of their new ventures, many people say, by way of undercutting the locals and they endured a great deal of prejudice for their hard work.

Immigrants were not made welcome and were treated with distrust and contempt by even the poorest and the most desperate. The unfortunate new citizens would often be publicly chastised, ridiculed and jostled mainly due to their unfamiliar dress and their misunderstood culture.

Eastern Europeans appeared from boats as they docked. Multitudes of those in hope of work and a better life, those in search of a sound and prosperous future; excited and full of positive notions, only to be disappointed and cast adrift into the sad fate of despondency. Resentful men with a limited grasp on the language and a hopeless destiny, sold roasted chestnuts from rickety carts or ripe oranges from broken crates. They played pitch and toss to pass the long days and stole money for a beer at nightfall.

There were many crimes committed under the veil of the smog, presumably linked to drink induced violence. The many random and severe beatings and rape of the pitiful and vulnerable street walkers, was sadly a regular occurrence. Many of the local constables turned a blind eye and seemed to give very little consideration to these unfortunate women as they were constantly subjected to the unchecked corruption of the night. The street walkers appeared to be looked on as rather a nuisance and were treated with distain; except by the men who carried a spare shilling or two in their pockets.

Children were born into poverty and sent, as young as five years of age, to sweep the narrow chimneys, or clean machines at the mills. Disconsolate men were reduced to tears as they were turned away from the docks, with no offer of assignment for a fair day's wage and exhausted mothers wept, with sheer desperation as they went about their daily chores and did their best with overworked hands and fingers that bled from constant scrubbing: Rats and strays picked through the rancid filth of the grimy gutters, in search of a tiny scrap to nibble on.

A potent risk of disease threatened, from the raw sewage that was flung from the cottages, then left to run along the cobbles and there was an acrid stench from the unclean clothes on the unwashed bodies of the families that could ill afford a bar of soap.

Homeless families huddled together in the narrow alleys, in a futile attempt to bring warmth to their thin bones. Women sorted through piles of rags, desperate and tearful as they searched for something suitable to cover the bare backs of their shivering off-spring. The curse of poverty invaded the streets, where the unhealthy pallor of the starving inhabitants, brought a pain and suffering too great to bear and inevitably led to their early demise.

I had no desire to visit the place but I was obliged to help my husband with his work.

I shuddered at the concept of the harsh lives lived in the grotesque neighbourhood and I coveted my fortunate existence, in the security of my comfortable house at the better end of town.

Chapter 4

Arthur

Chapter 4

Arthur

December 1887 was a Christmas I would not forget. It was bitterly cold and many people had frozen to death on the streets. The graves of the paupers were becoming fuller and fuller and there was nowhere to bury these poverty stricken unfortunates. My husband, Arthur, had toiled endlessly to save the people of the streets however; many of his efforts were futile.

The men continued drinking and chasing the brazen whores, despite the unbridled venereal diseases that were so easily contracted: They continued to expose themselves to the damned contamination, time after time and then endured it, until the treatment was either rendered ineffective, or the syphilis took too great a hold.

The women of the night appeared to be somewhat immune to the hideously cruel and debilitating symptoms of the diseases but the gentlemen suffered an agonising and shameful demise.

The whores simply aborted consequential foetuses then returned to their vulgar debauchery and continued to bring disease and pain to the good men of London town.

Wives sat in empty houses as their men afforded the lure of wantonness; readily available pleasure flowed in abundance; the unsolicited favours, provided by an array of buxom painted women, in rough brown dresses with big buttons and scant morals.

I had been a good wife; I loved my Arthur and was infinitely proud of his work. My beloved husband had gained great status in his profession, as a doctor and he had amassed a great fortune. He spent many of his spare hours looking after those who could not afford sound medical attention; his charity work was renowned and he had earned the greatest respect. He was a kind and considerate man and how I adored him.

Our life was comfortable and happy, some even envied us a little and there was nothing that could ever perturb us.

I often assisted my Arthur in his charitable work; I would gently hold the hands of the unfortunate, expectant young mothers, as the unwanted embryos were skilfully and humanely extracted from their bodies. The pitiful still-born babies, rescued from the heinous existence in the murky streets that held only poverty and suffering.

I sat at my dressing table as dear Arthur finished his whisky and placed the empty glass at the side of the bed. He looked pale and tired and I tenderly stroked his head as he drifted into a deep sleep. I thought that he may have been working too hard, as he had taken to spending long hours at his nightly meetings. I had remained at home, as my Arthur had considered the long conferences, far too tedious for me and was concerned that it would vex me. I climbed into our bed and held my darling husband as he slept in a silent repose.

I held him tightly to me, as it had been several months since he had required my wifely duties in the bedroom and I missed his tender touch. However, as I was five months gone I assumed he did not want to soil me with his impregnation, as he so clearly understood my discomfort.

The following morning Arthur remained in his bed, it was extraordinary, as he was always an early riser and I was alarmed.

By supper time, he had become extremely unwell and I called Dr Bridges to attend to him. His pale skin was covered in purple marks, he had large sores on his groin and he had a high fever and was shaking. He vomited copious amounts of bile and his head was hot to the touch. My husband was in the throes of a raging torment and my heart broke. I nursed my dear Arthur through the anguish of his encapsulating illness, I refused to leave his side for a second and I strived hard to believe, that he had caught the disease, through treating the unfortunate women in his care.

However, I had spent many hours helping him in his work and therefore; I knew the only way possible to contract it.

It was the early hours of New Years Eve in the year of 1887, when Dr Bridges had gently informed me that my dear Arthur had succumbed to double pneumonia, but, I had carefully nursed my dying husband and I knew only too well, the symptoms of his venereal disease.

We buried Arthur with full honours and the community grieved the loss of a great man. Two days after his funeral, I went into early labour and delivered my dead twins. My poor lifeless babies; cold and bloodied between my legs, a cruel and heartless fate that I deserved not. My dear husband my innocent children, my whole future suddenly taken from me and in the vilest of manners.

I was inconsolable and I yearned for the healing force that tears bring but I could not erase from my mind, the purple marks, or the wet sores that stained the bed sheets as Arthur lay fighting for his breath.

I sat for hours studying Arthur's medical notes, I had watched him work and I knew well how to use his tools. I noted the final names in a big red ledger that my husband kept open on his private desk, I discovered some names written separately at the back of the leather bound book but could not understand why they were there, or why payment had been noted, as services to the unfortunates had always been charitable. I contemplated the unusual, recent entries, for a considerable while but it was several weeks before it dawned on me.

I checked the ledger again and again. The payments were outgoing, not incoming. It was a nauseating revelation. No matter, I had time a plenty on my hands, I would see to it that Arthur had not died in vain and I committed myself to an appropriate revenge; one that would relinquish the soul of my dead husband and one that would send the foul perpetrators into the depths of hell itself.

The deaths of these vile whores would be the price to pay for my lost babies and my darling Arthur.

Chapter 5

Streetwalker

Chapter 5

Streetwalker

The lantern lighters and the constables on the beat, gathered collectively in the quiet corner of Mitre Square, They tipped their hats and politely wished me a good-day, as I handed out shillings to the old and the needy. The cobbled streets were grimy, they smelled of urine and I had to quickly swerve on several occasions, in order to avoid the chamber-pots as their contents were flung through open windows.

The bottom of my skirts had invariably become saturated and the heaviness of it was irritating and grit was dragging along underneath. However, it bothered me very little and I concentrated hard on mapping my escape route in my head, I continued to trudge deliberately through the murky and uneven streets, I had to, as I would have to remember how to find my way around in the dark during my next visit.

My feet hurt and the grit made them itchy and sore, but a little dirt was of no real consequence in the grand scheme of the things to transpire. My senses had heightened, with each painful step as my route through the narrow thoroughfare became defined.

The streets were fairly clear of the whores during the daytime, as most of the single ones, with no extra mouths to feed, would be sleeping off their drunken stupors; a short interlude in readiness for another quick tanner to be made under the cover of night. I made a note of the taverns and the quiet corners and archways that would provide good cover, for them to undertake their sinful work. I identified the dingy lodging houses that offered a bed for a sixpence and the hiding places that would conceal me as I went about my covert business.

I cautiously picked my way through small groups of children, dirty and bedraggled in their hand-me-down clothes. I stepped cautiously over the disgusting faeces left by several stray dogs; I tried to avoid the animals as much as was possible, in the worriment of receiving an unfriendly bite or of catching their fleas. Obstinate and vicious, snarling fiercely in an ungratified search for nourishment, as they fought their daily battle to survive.

Shady convicts and light-fingered children tried their luck at the many fruit, vegetable and flower stalls and the match sellers sat woefully on the kerbs hoping for a penny.

Rats scuttled into the gutters and bickered over tiny morsels of discarded, stale food. Malnourished babies with dirty faces lay in rickety, unattended prams outside the open front doors of their overcrowded and grubby terraced houses, their cries ignored by busy mothers.

A painfully thin cat hissed fiercely at me, as I passed by the window-sill it rested on and the sound of irate, scolding mothers and squabbling children resounded in the thick afternoon smog. It appeared I was in another world, I emptied my purse to the homeless and starving along the way, as I walked for hours until the sun began to set and the mist turned a heavier, darker grey as the light began to fade.

As I walked along the grimy pavements, I noticed that there were plenty of obscure places, the numerous nooks and crannies of the network of squares and alleyways, offered the most perfect hiding places and adequate concealment from those passing by, masking the outrageous goings on, the regular misdemeanours and the sins of the night.

I observed gentlemen's carriages as they were pulled to a halt outside the favourite haunts. Fine horses cantered to a stop and I watched as the cloaks of the elusive and deceitful men, caught on the protruding hinges and high steps as they alighted in undisguised haste; a minor irritation as they glanced furtively around them before disappearing into the cleaner and more organized and very exclusive, brothels and seedy clubs. The places run by madams, where the girls were looked after well, as long as they retained their looks.

What perilous entertainment for those, depraved enough to clamour for some better gratification, seeking out the company of the desperate young women, drinking and spreading their diseases with each spread of their legs.

The less wealthy men sauntered around in their tweeds and flat caps, seeking a weak beer and a cigarette and perhaps a quiet shrouded corner for their cheap little bit of ecstasy in the night. A shilling or two, or a fresh piece of fruit was a small price to pay for putting their health at risk, as they conducted their most dangerous business.

The lure of what was contained inside the drawers of the whores seemed irresistible to these men. I felt no pity for the women who used their broken bodies, to pay for a place to rest their heads, until the rise of the next unfortunate dawn. I despised the lewdness and the flannel petticoats the reckless girls hitched up, in readiness for a rough groin and fumbling fingers. A huge sea of smuttiness filled with a multitude of obscenities.

I scrutinized the scene around me and I wondered why these people, of seemingly low intellect, so uneducated and lacking in any ambition, survived their uninteresting existence, with no attempt to better themselves. They appeared to be content with their meagre lives on the surface of it all; but, who knows what thoughts or illusions of grandeur they had and would they ever reach their goals.

I realised that I had my work cut out, if I was going to be successful in my quest, however, I had become truly focussed and I was very determined. There appeared to be nothing too sinister to worry about in the streets during the daylight hours, but, I, alone, knew what darkness would bring to the inhabitants of this place.

I had taken my fill of Whitechapel for the time being and I had a strong desire to return to my home, so I dragged my heavy and soiled petticoats above my ankles and quickened my pace until I reached the iron gates of the park.

Chapter 6

Mary

Chapter 6

Mary

Quite a few weeks had passed since I had caused the demise of Martha. I had been practicing in the darkness, on some small animals, as it was imperative that I got it right this time. I had been rendered a little unsatisfied and I had need of absolution.

My first two attempts had been messy and slightly unprofessional and I was ashamed of my tackiness. It was time to redeem myself and to get the job done properly. I took Arthur's black cloak and checked the large pocket I had sewn into my skirt. The one that would hold safely, the soft leather wrap of sharp tools.

Everything appeared to be in order and I slipped out into the darkness. I celebrated the air of confidence about me, as I made my way to Whitechapel Road in the early hours of a cool August morning.

There were the usual revellers in the area and although I still retained an innate fear of being discovered, I knew the majority of the citizens would be too inebriated to notice me. I walked close to the walls of the brick buildings, and I hoped my long dark cloak gave me anonymity as I stalked my prey. The London mist was already in the air and although I felt a chill around me, I was grateful for the foggy curtain.

I soon located Mary; she was making her way towards the stables. As good a place as any, I suppose, if you are going to lie on the ground. The well-dressed young man accompanying her glanced shiftily around, as if he was afraid of detection as they disappeared out of sight.

I waited until the man had finished his noisy business with Mary, then I entered the stables. Mary had passed out on the floor, her skirt was still above her waist and I was ecstatic, as she had unwittingly prepared herself for me and I set to work.

I knelt at her side and slid Arthur's sharp surgeon's blade across her neck, it went in a bit deep and her head toppled forwards on to her chest, it startled me a bit but I pushed it back and thought no more about it as I sliced at the leathery skin around her abdomen. Her eyes were open and I found it slightly objectionable, as I did not want to be watched. I stuck the knife into her bloodied neck for a second time, I was merciless and the sharp knife ripped into her being with a force I was not aware I possessed. She flopped around with each vicious thrust of the tool and I silently screamed in my private rage.

I heard footsteps approaching, so I quickly made some small stabs to her torso and in her revolting pelvis. I had not had time to locate her ovaries, I had so wanted to take them to burn and destroy. I took instead the cheap ring from her finger, it would have to do. I glanced down at the lifeless corpse and checked my tools were safely tucked into my pocket, before stepping back into the darkness.

I crept quietly away from the bloodied scene, silent and unobserved, as usual, and I tip-toed past the shabby little two storey cottages then down towards the imposing brick warehouses of Bucks Row. The dim glow of the lamp-light skimmed my head as I passed quietly along the pavement; too small and insignificant to warrant a second glance.

I heard the sound of shouting and turned to see two men coming from the direction of the stables. An adrenaline rush seared through my body and it felt wonderful, I was beyond all suspicion, as who would imagine it? A mere woman of such bold strength and she with a fine knowledge of the human anatomy. I had done a great deal better this time and I would do even better, the next time. However, it was clear, that this time I had triumphed and although I was missing a trophy to burn, I had a ring to cast down into the Thames. It would be a small consolation, I know, but the act of disposing of it would please me greatly. The cheap trinket had meant not a thing to me, except to re-live the pleasure of tearing it away from the loathsome, limp hand of Mary.

I pulled my cape around me and turned back towards the stables. To all around me I was a normal, inquisitive individual, in the midst of a crowd of morbid onlookers, shocked and traumatised by the gruesome scene before them, however, not me, they were wrong, I was a phantom, an enigma of huge proportions, I was unstoppable.

I wiped the palms of my hands across my parched mouth, unwittingly smearing the blood of Mary all over my face, it tasted of metal as I licked my lips, and I knew that I was indeed much stronger than I had ever dreamed to give myself credit for.

With the pretence of a coy whisper had come the slice of a throat, it was a messy business and in its profound lifelessness, a body became very heavy to move. It was labourious but what joy I felt as I worked.

Another worthless soul had been successfully committed into the arms of the devil. I truly was becoming of great befuddlement to the police. I heard screams calling for the police to end the reign of Jack the Ripper. I heard whistles and the sound of racing footsteps, Women shrieked in fear and men shouted in their anger. The police lashed out with their truncheons, confused and irritated, as I continued my slow walk home. It was the moment that I knew I had become invisible and deadly.

I could now proceed with very little fear, as after all, were the police constables not looking for a man, perhaps a doctor, or a butcher, a Jew or an immigrant, many an elusive suspect would be accused.

Thank you Jack, as you are such a good friend, donned in your top hat and your cloak. Your letters continue to assist me in my quest. The blame is on your own head Jack and the search for you will continue, however futile.

Chapter 7

Boss

Chapter 7

Boss

Look Sir at the postmark, take a note, Sir, and a quiet contemplation is required. The veritable solution is not to be concealed. A sound falsehood and a game played by a senseless prankster: I wrote the scolding words with great relish. The newspaper boss would not take a look too closely at my letters, but would concentrate on those that were, so foolish and so maliciously contrived by a charlatan.

The very idea of a scoundrel such as Jack the Ripper will sell many papers and the titillation is profound.

Not so a sight to behold, rather a ploy to confuse your reporters and readers. The letters placed on your desk are false, and a lone and idiotic vagabond plays games at your expense, Sir. Continue with your ineptitude and I will carry on, unhindered, there is still plenty of work to be done and it will be done at my hand alone. Seek carefully a man called Jack, as the one to be put to question will remain free. The letters by the hand of another will not give forth a reasonable clue. Be wary of the ill fared games of a common man, as another night of spilled blood is soon to be upon us and the red ink is of no value, as it hinders your thoughts.

Be gone with your nonsensical cartoons of a man in top hat and a cloak, vanishing in and out of the shadows, as you seek just a simple woman dressed as a servant girl. A clever thing, don't you think? I stood up from the writing desk and gathered my thoughts. It was therapeutic and the words flowed from my hands as I scribbled them on to the parchment in a controlled anger.

The torture of the whores is my bliss. I feign to delight in their suffering and I am duty bound to continue in my quest, even if it is under the guise of Jack.

We will seek redemption back to back in our own way and I Sir, will be triumphant. The ink blotted the words as I pressed the quill down too hard in my fury. I knew the words would never be read by the newspaper boss but it was my release. It was my way of confessing, my admission of a crime that would never be revealed.

I felt the tension ease away as each word was spelled. I had no intention of sending them but the letters eased my soul and I felt a great satisfaction as I burned them in the hearth in the drawing room.

I held the notion that I would never be caught, as I was fighting against a regime of masculinity, caught up in a desire to be right and the urge to catch Jack the Ripper would take on the face of adversity. I had conquered my insecurities under the veil of the egos of men and I was in a perfect hiding place, under the very noses of those that looked on me as gentle and meek.

I was an unassuming mass murderer, one solely responsible for some of the most heinous and indescribable atrocities that would ever be committed, and I was the elusive shadow they feared. A strong and resilient sinner but to all who knew me, I was a heartbroken little widow, so grieved and so lonely!

I poked around at the charred remains of the parchment in the fireplace until they turned to dust, then I called for the maid to bring me some refreshment.

Chapter 8

Maid

Chapter 8

Maid

Polly quickly appeared through the door, her pretty face had its usual expectant and accommodating smile and I beckoned her towards me. I asked her to bring us some tea and to sit for a while.

My sweet little maid looked slightly bemused but did as I bid and soon returned with a tray of hot tea and some of cook's home-made shortbread. I gestured for her to sit, and then I poured the liquid into the bone china cups Arthur and I had chosen together. We spoke of ribbons and gowns. I held her tiny chaffed hands in mine and kissed her rosy cheek.

Polly appeared slightly taken aback by my behaviour but I assured her, that I simply wanted to display my appreciation for all her hard work and for looking after me when my Arthur had died. I told her I was blessed with the help she gave to me, in my time of great sorrow and thanked her for caring for me so well after the terrible loss of my tiny babies. It was pure honesty on my part, as the dear little maid had worked her fingers to the bone, to provide my utmost comfort and my behaviour had been so sullen and discourteous, that I had failed to show my gratitude.

I felt no need to worry her and I was sure Agnes would take her under her wing in a time of need. My cook was very fond of Polly, as was I. She was such a sweet and charming girl, who had served us well and had gained our absolute trust and respect.

I had somewhat neglected her dedication, as I strived to continue my mission and I hoped her next mistress would be good to her and treat her with the kindness she so deserved. She had shown great concern for me, as her employer and I appreciated her faith in me.

I asked Polly if she was walking out with a young man and she confided in me, that she had befriended a young man called Jim, a sound young lad who worked at the stables in Lime Street. She was to meet him in the park at the end of the road, at two-o-clock the following afternoon and she was wearing her new lace-up boots. I demanded she choose a gown from my closet and she timidly tried some on, first a pale blue one with lace down the centre, then a deep pink one with a cream bustle and deep sleeves. I decided to offer them both for her keeping and delighted in her shy merriment. I also gave her a matching bonnet with ribbon strings and a dainty parasol with cream embroidering all over it. I lied, when I said that the gowns were ill fitting on me and I felt no desire to alter them.

We chatted a little more, then I sent her to her room, as she had many chores to do before lunch the following day and not only that, she had to be looking her best to meet Jim.

Dear Charlotte or Lottie, as she liked to be called, was a friend of Polly and she came twice a week to polish the brass and black lead the hearth. A good worker and eager to please, sweet in her nature, with never a moment of complaint; her aunt managed the workhouse and she treated her young niece with distain. Perhaps a few guineas would fare her well and a pretty dress and a bonnet for good measure. A fitting letter of recommendation and a bond for no less than fifty pounds would be pleasing to her as a parting gift.

I undressed and climbed into my bed, I had several things to attend to, I was well aware that New Years Eve would be fast approaching and there was much work to be done. Four thirty on the 31st December was a very important date for me.

Chapter 9

Annie

Chapter 9

Annie

I watched from the shadows, as Annie chatted to her friends in Hanbury Street. I had followed her for the entire evening but she had acquired no luck in her quest to earn money for her bed. It was getting quite late and I was concerned that the September sun was about to rise. I was about to retire when she stopped her chat and moved to the rear of the narrow street, presumably to find somewhere to lay her head, or drink her rum.

I followed closely by and Annie turned to face me as I approached her, she asked me if I could spare a couple of bob and as I reached into my skirt, she gave me a huge expectant smile. A doomed smile, from an unsuspecting wretch, she stepped towards me just before I thrust the knife into her scrawny throat. The look of surprise as the life drained from her eyes encapsulated my being. It was a fine moment watching her life ebb from her, I stared at her for a second before pushing her down against the wooden fence, I had my tools ready and I swiftly lifted up her skirt and sliced open her abdomen, I fumbled around for a short while, I could not readily distinguish her womb, due to her soft plumpness and because of the amount of blood that was pooling in that area. I finally located the trophy and sliced it away from her. I put it in a leather bag that was tied around my waist.

I decided to take her ovaries and bladder too, just for good measure and I yanked out her intestines, they were long and tangled, so they irritated me and I draped them over her right shoulder, they felt slimy and warm and they reminded me of snakes. I turned her face to the left, as the sight of it perturbed me, I did not want to see it. I scattered her meagre belongings alongside her and covered her open cuts with some torn away skin. The remainder, I shoved over her other shoulder. Annie was into her late forties but she looked sixty. I stared at my handiwork and leaned against the wall. I felt nothing at all for the insignificant wretch at my feet. It was a bitter-sweet juncture as my emotions had long since abandoned me and I was void of conscience. I felt a wave of elation as I celebrated my successful endeavour. My trophy was safe in the bag at my side and a good job had been done.

This time there had been no interruption, I was in no rush to leave the scene, as I was in fact, enjoying the vision before me. The now familiar heady rush overcame me and I stumbled backwards. It was like a surge of honour that encompassed my soul. The dawn was breaking and I knew I must take heed and leave the scene before the light of the September morning was to reveal me.

I couldn't resist the temptation and before I left, I managed to cut away the front of her pubis. That heinously rancid pad of flesh, the softness that had cushioned my husband's swollen groin, as he pounded his manhood against her.

Annie's womb would burn brightly in the hearth and I looked forward to watching the flesh contract as the heat consumed it. The whore's purse, her uterus, it was the vessel that had perhaps so cruelly expelled the countless unwanted little babies. How unfair, that these women, so insignificant but so fruitful, could chose not to carry full term their infants and mine were both dead, lost through no choice of my own.

Expelled without consideration for their tiny souls and forever gone, with the most excruciating pain to my heart. Stolen by the disease that engulfed my family.

Stillborn twins, the consequence of complications of venereal disease, spread from the disgusting harlots, first to my husband and then to me, the effects of it causing my womb to contract and eject the two beating hearts within it.

The filth I had contracted from the vulgar and verminous women of the night, made me sick to my insides and I grieved for my husband and my dead babies. I grieved but I also craved vengeance. I picked my way back through the most impoverished and crime ridden streets of Whitechapel and sauntered slowly in my triumph until I reached my home. I had given the servants the whole day off, as I wished to be alone as I drew my soothing bath. There would now be no further defilement from the loins of Annie and I was content.

I slipped into the tepid water and sponged the thick red liquid from my body, then, I plaited my hair and lay on the huge empty bed and closed my eyes in a deep sleep.

I dreamed of my babies and a life denied to them, I pictured them growing up, fine and healthy and I imagined them running in a wide field of deep green grass, with my Arthur watching over them; safe in a place far away from the stinking streets and foul beings. A happy place; where I would find them when the time was right. Meanwhile, I was to continue on with my atonement. There was still much work to be done and winter was fast approaching.

Two beautiful souls lost by the action of an unfaithful husband and the diseases of the sordid whores that tempted his lust. Whichever individual it was, that infected him, is of no concern to me, there were many to choose from and they would pay for my pain in unison. Time and patience were the things I possessed in abundance and I was becoming more confident and skilled with Arthur's tools, of which there were plenty. The mission had started off rather clumsily but I was gaining my confidence and getting a lot better at my task and I knew I would soon finish it.

I struck through 3 of the names written in the back of the red ledger that belonged to my dead husband.

Chapter 10

Jack

Chapter 10

Jack

What is this profanity the newspapers are telling of? A letter, said written in blood and sent by the hand of a murderer. Which fiend is this, it is not I? The letter is signed by Jack, who is Jack and for what reason does he take the credit for my work.

I threw the newspaper to the ground. The very insolence of it dumbfounded me. A lie was told and those who would believe it should be ashamed. Was it not the case that the Whitechapel citizens were fast becoming void of the wanton whores, that polluted their depraved community, and I, myself would seek to discontinue in my errand, rather than give credence, to one so dishonest.

My mission was marred, Jack! Whoever you are, refrain so, from soiling my quest with your innocuous falsehood! I calmed myself and prepared a nice cup of tea. I mused over the letter in the papers and it did not amuse me in the least, however, it soon presented a new concept to me and I realised that these fanciful letters could easily be held in my favour. The foolhardy impostor was an unexpected cover that I must use to my advantage. Therefore, I should not fret so, instead, I must use the guise of this man to blanket me in my continued work. This new development, laid bare the chance of mistaken identity, as, after all, if the police searched for a man in a cape and a tall hat, how then would they find little old me!

The idiocy of man, a furtive ally had been duly created with the stroke of a pen. I knew what I must do and I put to work.

Arthur's clothes still held his faint aroma, I cradled them closely to me and closed my eyes as I buried my face in the linen, but still no tears were shed, despite the searing agony in my soul. It was difficult to feel the grief of a lost husband, when the circumstances had brought such pain and sorrow. I craved the life I once had and the ache in my heart only intensified, with each item I set aside.

The tall, black top-hat, had been carefully stored in a large box with deep red velvet lining. I tried it on my head and although it was slightly large, it sat perfectly. The heavy black cape with the tie strings at the neck required just a few inches of shortening and I was sure I would find the time to see to it, before I embarked on my next errand. I carefully placed it on the floor and lifted the lid of the wooden trunk at the end of my bed.

I searched for the shiny black cane, the one with the silver top cast in the shape of a horse; it had been a gift from my father in law and was made of fine ebony. It had given Arthur a great deal of pleasure and had been the envy of his colleagues. I held it aloft and swung it with all my force to the floor. The silver top flew across the room and landed in the far corner. I would deal with that later, as I was keen to begin work on my new disguise.

I was not about the business of simply extinguishing a life, I was also intent on removing the trophies, the ones that portray only the female gender. The internal atrocities, those that remain unseen with the eyes but will retain the abhorrence of an insidious venereal disease: The fleshy masses, that hold a malady so devastating and so virulent that with just the hitch of a skirt, was so easily transmitted. I took a white handkerchief from my pocket, I had forgotten all about it and blood and saliva had dried on to the linen. The marks from Annie's teeth had made small indents in the material and it was still crumpled from where I had forced it into her mouth. I slipped it back inside my pocket and sat at the hearth.

The remnants of the whore's womb lay charred in the ashes and I poked at it with the toasting fork. It was just like a piece of coal and I left it for the maid to attend to.

I checked the newspapers avidly there was much ado about Jack the Ripper, people thought he might be a doctor, the wounds he so skilfully cut, they said. The wounds I cut methinks! It was a very interesting concept and I surged with pride that my work was so well regarded.

There was a great public uproar from the ordinary people, who lived in fear of the murderer roaming their streets at night. I heard that the doctors were shouted at and their bags bullishly searched, as they went about their usual business and I heard that there were riots and fights and that no man was safe from any accusation, or adverse reaction to my crimes.

I held no concept of the fear and peril the ladies of the night were forced to endure. All that mattered was that one of them had infected my darling Arthur and there was no sense to it. A man so moralistic and of a kindness beyond comprehension, there could be left no other explanation, he had been bewitched by the wantonness of a female. How so, was puzzling, as he had often complained about the stench of unwashed genitals and the risk of infection.

I pulled the big cloth sack from the box beneath my bed and donned the simple grey cotton dress. It was still grimy and had blood stains all over the sleeves and skirt, however, it would give the illusion of poverty should I need to merge into the crowds. An illegal abortionist, perhaps, or a butcher's assistant. The blood and grime on my dress could easily be explained this way. Not much notice would be brought.

Young women were often beaten and then thrown at the mercy of the streets and left to wander in misery; as to return to their homes, resulted in more abuse. I rubbed horse manure into my skin to give the illusion of lack of hygiene. I slipped the soft leather wrap containing my husband's tools into the large pocket I had sewn into the skirt of the plain grey dress. I kicked off my fine stockings and forced on some old leather boots, before I pulled Arthur's formidable cape tightly around me and donned his top hat.

I would begin the night as a fine gentleman and end it as an insignificant servant. I had no fear of Jack, as Jack was simply a writer of letters and a fanciful fool. Where lies, this burden of proof Jack? I think our game continues.

Will you finally un-mask me? I suspect not. Is it not true that your letters come from Hell? Sir, it is a place I have visited and I know you not from there!

There had been a few more letters and it amused me. The notorious East End, the place crammed with phantoms and whores is hardly a place where wealthier citizens are readily exposed to the sordid underside of society. A letter writer, perhaps a man in a cutaway coat, dark trousers and a round hat, one would expect to recognise as a reporter, roaming with a notebook in hand and merging into gathering crowds. A martyr to my cause, you write, Sir, in an unusual manner, to gain enjoyment and I dispose of the whores for the same reason.

Methinks the editors absurdly betray an inner knowledge, one provided only to the police and the press. A veritable wave of bogus information; freely dispersed into the minds of those surviving the cobbled streets, stories inciting fear and worry.

Thank you Jack, for a good citizen takes forth the blame for another and aids my sleep. Poor deluded Jack, let me wish you well on your journey of self importance.

Chapter 11

Liz

Chapter 11

Liz

The rain beat heavily down and I debated whether or not to venture out in it. It was typical weather for late in September and Arthur's large cape was heavy, I feared it would hinder me if it were to get wet. The top hat was of no use in the pouring rain and I searched for another, more suitable one to cover my hair.

My fine locks pulled back easily into a knot and could be hidden well by a soft hat. The false moustache was itchy but I kept it on as it gave me a truly masculine appearance, despite my lacking of height. Five foot five was average for a woman but noticeably small for a man. I assumed the trim moustache would counteract that, should I be spotted.

Berner Street was, as usual, filled with the raucous laughter of the street girls as they plied their wares, and drunken and bawdy men searching for their five minutes of ecstasy, lingered on street corners waiting for a wink. The gas lamps emitted a dim light that cast wide shadows and made the grim surroundings barely discernible.

Turning into Duttfield Yard, I caught sight of one of the prostitutes there, she had just pleasured her client with her mouth; she was well known for that particular speciality. The notorious whore was missing of several teeth and her skills in the art of fellatio made her a popular fare. She was constantly busy; however, no-one had any desire to kiss her, as her lips had a foul flavour from the constant swallowing of ejaculated mess.

I searched for Liz but she was nowhere to be found, I walked twice around her usual haunts, before starting on my way back to Whitechapel Road. It was just as I walked across Commercial Street, by a stroke of luck, I caught a sight of Liz sauntering in the opposite direction. She wore her skirt hitched up so as not to drag it on the floor and a shawl was pulled tightly around her shoulders. Her hair was stuck to her head and it gave her the look of a bedraggled witch. The aborted plan was restored and I turned back towards the yard and waited for her to catch up with me. I heard her singing as she approached me and I undid the leather wrap in my pocket.

My cape was drenched and I felt so cold from the incessant rain that I began to tremble. It was well past midnight and I had been outside for hours. The wanton women cared little for the rain, a bed for the night depended on their trade. The lodging houses had no room for those that could not pay and the whores had little desire to sleep at the kerb. On a night such as this, it was prudent to work quickly and get inside from the elements. Many had succumbed to pneumonia and T.B. and a warm bed was payment enough for a hard day's work.

Liz was tall, she held an imposing figure and as I approached her, she raised her arm to the light to identify me. I lashed out at her, catching her underarm and she bent forward, I used the cover of darkness to creep behind her and as she turned around, I slashed at her neck, I did it twice and she made a strange gurgling sound as she fell to the floor, it was very dark and as I went about my business, I could hear voices from the working men's club door as it opened and a shard of light lit up the square. I hesitated and an unpleasant tight feeling welled up in my throat as the dread of revelation consumed me.

I edged back into the shadows as two men passed nearby, just missing the lifeless body of Liz as she lay defunct, in newly executed oblivion. It had been a near miss, as I was slow in my movements due to the rain soaking into my cloak and burdening me. I decided to remove the silky lining from it, on my return home, as it served only to hinder me. I took no trinket from Liz, she had nothing about her person and there were people beginning to gather at the club. I had started my work far too near the gates and had become in fear of detection, I had extinguished her life and that would have to do for the moment.

An unfinished piece of work lays heavily on me and although I was soaked through, I had a great desire to remain focussed. I still had the cover of night, which would last for several hours and would offer me another opportunity to locate a subsequent objective. There would be sufficient time in order to make good my escape and I made my way homewards to gather my notion, perhaps I had time for a second attempt.

I removed the sticky blood from my hands and I settled for a while with the calming aid of a hot cup of tea, before I was of the mind to carry out the next task. There were still enough hours of darkness to use as camouflage and I was in a state of unrest. I was sick of interruptions and the inability to reach a conclusion. I reached for the black cape and top hat and I slipped back out into the night.

I couldn't help but to wonder, how many wealthy and influential gentlemen would have crossed paths with these desperate whores of Whitechapel and what wistful truths had been revealed in their demise. What tales were told at the private gentlemen's clubs, for surely the reticent and filthy degradation, of their strange and uninhibited fantasies would become apparent there and freely discussed under the strong influence of a glass of the best single malt: The secret gatherings of exemplary men, secure in a clandestine atmosphere, in the safe and blameless haven where they were free to share their transgressions.

I wondered what stories Arthur had told as he sipped his whisky from the crystal tumblers. My dearest husband, a man of such great status; were his evenings spent, so raucously spinning the tales of his base defilement. I felt a surge of liquid rise in my throat as I entered the gates into the park.

Chapter 12

Catherine

Chapter 12

Catherine

The walk along to Butchers row took a bit longer than I expected and even though I had torn the heavy lining from my cape, the weight of it still confounded me. I had discovered, by means of idle gossip that Catherine Eddowes, had been thrown into a cell to sleep off her drunken apathy. It was a common event and the inebriated women were most often thrown back out on to the streets on awakening.

I had no need to comb the dark streets, as on this occasion, I knew exactly where to find my quarry. I sat at a bench alongside Mitre Square, it was cold and damp but I waited with easy patience until I spotted Catherine.

The three city detectives, cleverly in the process of orchestrating the covert patrol, failed to deceive me and I tottered past them under the guise of an unfortunate. One of them enquired about my cape and I told them I had been given it as favour for my services. The explanation pleased him well enough and the three men went on their way. The inspector at Scotland Yard had organized extra patrols and I knew that I had just under fifteen minutes between each one, to complete my task.

Catherine swayed from side to side as she walked ungainly into the square. I continued watching as she solicited a young man wearing a flat cap. He slapped one of her buttocks and they disappeared into the south west corner of the square, where it was darkest. I crept close and observed the copulation. It was a squalid act, rampant and debauched, bestial, like animals out in the wild.

The act was soon accomplished, with the man emitting a loud whine, such as you would expect to hear from a wounded dog. Catherine then pulled down her skirt and held out a grubby expectant hand. The gentleman handed her some coins, then buttoned up his breeches before tipping his hat and disappearing into the darkness. Catherine leaned up against the wall and I waited until the policeman had walked on.

A Bobby out on his beat, an unsuspecting figure of authority, not so a deterrent but a heedless individual in search of Jack the Ripper, he was unaware of my presence as he slowly passed by an imminent murder.

Catherine Eddowes had a pretty face, the kind of face that would draw the lust of many a decent man. I counted the seconds in my head as I set to work on her. She did not see me coming as I swiftly pulled down her bonnet and slit her pretty white throat. The now familiar gurgling sound, as a windpipe separated and released the air, excited me, and I felt the adrenaline rush to my head. I enjoyed the thrill of it but I could not revel in it, too much, as the seconds were counting down and my time was limited.

Catherine's throat gaped open and blood was pooling around her as I sliced through her abdomen looking for a trophy. It was rather a messy affair, and I was required to wipe my hands on my skirt constantly, as her intestines ruptured and created a mess; so much so, that it was difficult to work. I threw the elongated, slimy mass over her shoulder and managed to locate her left kidney. I chopped at it then popped it into my leather pouch, I thought that perhaps I would get cook to make a pie with it. I used her shawl to mop up some of the blood, the garment was rather fine and it appeared far too extravagant for someone of her status; so I assumed it was either a gift from one of her affluent gentlemen callers, or perhaps it had been stolen. The pretty shawl could not have become hers in any other manner, as the impoverished women wore predominantly cotton and flannel or wool. I threw the garment to the floor as it was of no consequence to me.

Catherine lay with her eyes open, how dare she; what vulgarity, to be so rude and stare at me so! I nicked her eyelids and cut off the end of her pert little nose, then I slit her eyelids so that, her eyes, sightless and grey, could no longer wink as she plied her rancid wares. I stamped on her face and stood aside to check that no more sound would emit from the gaping hole that was once her mouth.

I cut a little V shape in each of her pretty cheeks; it was a mark to be remembered, a permanent indication of the filthy venereal diseases the ladies of the night carried. I popped the tip of her nose in my pouch, I was aware that I had very little time left before the next patrol, so I snipped at the edge of her ear, just for the novelty of it, before melting into the night and making my escape through to St James Place. I walked away unnoticed and left the body of Catherine Eddowes, sprawled in a sea of her own blood.

I heard the night watchman blow loudly and erratically on his whistle. I imagined him running to Jewry Street to alert the doctor. Too late, I was done and Catherine is bereft of her miserable life. Perhaps she should thank me for releasing her from her sordid and miserable existence. I had no idea how she had enjoyed her life, all I knew, was, it was now over. I crept along the walls of the brick buildings on my way to solace. All the newspapers would say it was Jack the Ripper. Believe what you may, perhaps Jack will furnish you with a letter about it, he will say he threw her clothes up over her waist and cut her body to pieces. Jack is the provider of lies, as the truth sits only with me.

I arrived home and cleansed the stains of my work from my body and hid away my dirty clothes. I sat at my husband's desk and struck through another name in the big red ledger, then lay on the big wooden bed and was soon fast asleep.

I was gradually working through my list of possibilities and I would be thorough in my proposal. I heard that Jack had sent more letters: I had no tender words for the impostor and was of a mind; that should our paths ever cross; then perhaps I would be inclined to take my hatpin to his dishonest black eyes. The elusive Jack the Ripper deserved nothing except dismissal.

Chapter 13

Jane

Chapter 13

Jane

I considered myself to be very fortunate; I enjoyed a luxurious life with my darling husband of four blissfully happy years. The day had recently come, when I could disclose the news that I was with his child. I had already visited the doctor, at my husband's insistence and we had become delighted in the revelation that I was to be blessed with twins.

I was approaching my twenty fifth birthday and life was very good. My husband, Arthur, was an eminent doctor in the East end of London. He worked in a private clinic during the day and in his spare time, would treat the unfortunates living in the squalor of poverty stricken Whitechapel. His charitable work had earned him the greatest respect and he enjoyed the finest accolade.

I would often accompany my Arthur as he tended to the misadventures of the street ladies, their bodies battered and frail, from years of abuse and hunger, never failed to astound me. The resilience in their eyes, dared anyone to pity them, as they lay with legs extended, stripped of all decency as the unwanted embryos were extracted from their loins. The tragic result, of a life set against the mercy of the cruel streets, with not a mattress to sleep on, unless you possessed a few shillings.

The only way the women could survive, was to sell the only commodity they had available. It was a sorry situation and one that had very little reasonable conclusion. A repetitive and sordid tragedy to be unravelled and lamented: Many dirty hands were gently stroked by my own, as I held them tightly, whilst the frightened and forsaken women cried out in their agony, with desperation and remorse. Their plight saddened me greatly and I could not help but to compare my own life with theirs.

Growing up, I had very few friends. As an only child, I had soon learned to be content with my own company and I found it difficult to be in the presence of the other children, especially those that were given things, instead of time, as their selfishness irritated me and I could not comprehend the logic of it. To create hugely labourious tantrums over inanimate trinkets, or light scolding, was of the greatest entertainment to me and this source of discontent, would often cause a rift between my parents and theirs, as they cried more when I laughed.

I had, however, been very fortunate, in that my Nanny had spent hours on end playing board games, singing and helping me organise my dolls house. We adored each other and we spent many a happy hour playing in the garden or at the park. My Nanny, Grace, was barren, she had been left destitute by her gambling and philandering husband, he had kicked her unborn child from her belly and she had been destined for the workhouse.

It was sad affair and a fate most common, however, my mother had taken her into our employ as a wet nurse for me, at first, but, as she fitted into the family unit so well and obviously doted on me, they had offered her sole charge of me. My parents travelled often and had very little time for bringing up a child. Grace was a perfect solution. I conquered my insecurities with my faithful nanny at my side and I loved her dearly.

Grace is responsible for my success and fortitude in this world; she taught me how to sustain myself, her philosophy on life was simple: Our lives are like a mountain stream it begins with a steady trickle, but, eventually goes where it can find its own path and not where we may want it to go. Grace believed that God had no sense of humour; she was convinced that everyone had his blessing but would have to figure it out along the way.

My nanny taught me right from wrong, of course, but my strict parents would have been horrified at some of her theories, I knew that without her steady hand and resolute patience, I would have the same morals as the spoiled brats, so ungrateful for their privileged lives.

Grace now has a delightful family of her own, she married a widowed friend of my father and she is more than content in the role of nurturing her new stepchildren. We were regularly in touch and I was content in the knowledge that she had found new happiness. I loved Grace with all my heart and I knew she loved Arthur and me.

My closet of fine clothes, shoes and hats was enviable, we attended many high end and society events and were friends with some of the most influential and respected individuals. Our calendar was full and our company was highly regarded, and there were not many parties we were excluded from.

I often donated my jewellery to the thrift shops, in the hope that some benefit would reach the bellies of the hungry and Arthur would take medicine and clean water to the streets, during his charitable visits. In a life so privileged, I had found my fulfillment.

From the very beginning, I had failed to stomach the coy whispers and provocative behaviour of the unfortunates, I was very proud of the work Arthur did and I tried to ignore the brazen taunts as we toiled in the deprived abodes, however, once a young girl had pleaded with me to take her home to my master, she said he would pay three shillings for a buxom one like her. I cried but I did not know if it was out of disgust or fear that my master was enticed.

Life in the uncertainty of the Whitechapel corner was a far cry from a life I enjoyed and I put my heart and soul into helping those less fortunate than myself. Many of the influential doctors gave their time, to aid the curb of unwanted infants left to die in the streets. Children lost, before they were even born but saved from a life of hardship and misery. I prayed that I would never have a need to compromise, in the collision of our worlds

Home life consisted of a large house near the park. We enjoyed the services of two maids, a cook and Arthur had a personal valet that he trusted with his papers and all his personal business. We possessed our own two horses and a carriage that Arthur would use for his visits to the clinic and to the private gentlemen's club for his many nightly meetings. We had enjoyed several discussions on the benefits of employing a suitable nanny for our forthcoming babies and had started to plan the appropriate selection process.

During the nights Arthur spent at the club, I would play bridge, or sit quietly at the piano, I played rather well; however, my husky voice did not compliment me. A lot of my time was taken up with cross stitch; I would lose myself for hours in the pretty linens and coloured cottons, and I created pictures on small oval wooden frames. Arthur had put some on the bedroom wall for me and they were a source of great enjoyment. My little works of art, I called them! Arthur said they were delightful.

We considered ourselves to be extremely fortunate, we had an effortless and most affluent lifestyle, we enjoyed the wealth around us with relish and were both very well respected in the community. I adored my husband and he adored me. We craved for nothing else.

We had married on New Year's Eve in 1883, I was almost twenty and Arthur had turned twenty nine. At four thirty p.m. our vows to each other were celebrated with a soft kiss and a narrow gold band. I wore an exquisite dress of royal blue; it had cream frills at the bodice and a bustle of cream at the back. My new husband told me that I was the most beautiful woman he had ever seen and he was proud to have me at his side. We spent our honeymoon at a sweet old cottage, tucked away in the countryside, near the town of Windsor. It was indeed the happiest time of my life. I closed the shutters each night and learned how to please Arthur.

Our families had brought us together, my father was a successful shipping merchant and my mother was heavily involved in many children's charities, her activities in the community, kept her busy whilst my father was absent on his business. My parents had become great friends with the parents of Arthur and it had been by this fortitude, I met my husband.

I loved Arthur from the moment we were introduced and I knew he would treasure me. He told me that I reminded him of a favourite aunt, he had adored as a child and the love he felt then, had transcended to me as soon as he saw me. He missed her terribly and I appeared to fill the void she had left in his heart.

In total contrast to my mother, I despised my husband's business trips; the lonely nights without Arthur at my side seemed to unsettle me. They did not occur too often but, on occasions I would fret and pace the bedroom. I placed my hand on my swollen abdomen and the sweetest anticipation of impending mother-hood consumed me. I peered through the heavy drapes and into the dim light of the street but all was quiet. I lay on the bed until I heard the key turn in the lock of the front door and I knew my husband was home.

I was not overtly fond of the full act of copulation, I considered it uncomfortable and rather messy, however, Arthur had his husbandly needs and as his dutiful wife, it was my place to indulge him so. The last time I had pleased him with my mouth, I had noticed an unusual sore on his groin and a foul taste at his hood. I urged him to work less hard, as I did not want him to neglect himself, or become ill and I was concerned that he may be spending too much time in his starchy clothes. Once Arthur had relaxed and released the liquid tension inside him, I prepared him a warm bath and a clean robe for his comfort. We lay silently, in each other's arms and my tired husband drifted into a restless sleep.

That had been the last time I had felt my husband inside me and I retched violently at the memory of it.

I brought my mindfulness back to the cold November night of 1888 and carefully ran my forefinger along the edge of the sharp blade, the one I had recently washed the blood from.

Chapter 14

Cook

Chapter 14

Cook

My faithful cook, Agnes Brown, had been with our family for many years and I was confident that she would find alternative employment. Dearest Agnes was without question, a most genial and hardworking individual, she was held by us all, in the highest esteem and I was certain, that any other household would be infinitely more than delighted to have her.

Our big house was continually filled with the aroma of freshly baked bread and pies, Agnes held the most kindly and pleasant demeanour. One of her most wonderful traits was her calmness and I had not once heard a raised voice during her time with us. She had turned out to be such an absolute treasure and I would, so, miss my plump and friendly cook, with her pink cheeks and ample bosom; I had a great affection for her. I had been so fortunate in my choice of staff and I hoped I had managed to show them my gratitude.

I had already managed to discover through the grapevine, that is, that Doctor and Mrs Hughes were considering a new housekeeper, as theirs had recently become with child and her notice had been accepted. I would offer my finest recommendation, when the time was right, and I had very little doubt, that the new position would become the charge of Agnes.

I made my way to the kitchen, Agnes sat carefully peeling potatoes, she glanced up as I entered her domain and I gestured for her to sit herself back down. The kettle was already boiling on the stove and I made us both a cup of hot tea. I sat for over an hour with Agnes and we spoke of old times and of new. We toasted her fresh tasty crumpets on the open fire, and topped them with salted butter. I had first worried about her, as she had become widowed, shortly before we had taken her into our employ, but, she had settled in extremely well; I think she was glad of the company and a place to stay and her skills in the kitchen were second to none. Dear Arthur had particularly loved her hot drop scones and home-made jams and she had revelled in his constant praise of them. Her smile radiated as he cleared his plate of every morsel and winked as he wiped his mouth.

A jolly woman, of great stature, Agnes smelled of yeast and onions, she was quite simple in the head but gifted in the ways of a good kitchen, a buxom woman of few words, with a delicate soul, my cheerful cook, was a beacon of light in this dark and ugly world of ours. This world, where honesty and integrity was selective; this hostile world, where the faces in front of yours, were served, shrewdly and coldly at the expense of those that were out of momentary sight.

I enjoyed my discussion with Agnes; so much so, that the late hour deceived us and we had became weary with our talk. We wished each other a good night and made haste to bed. I said I would take my breakfast late, as I knew she would fret. I decided to give Agnes my favourite gold chain, the one with the delicate oval locket enclosing a pink pearl. I knew she coveted it, as she often complimented it, whenever

I wore it at my throat. I pictured my dear Agnes wearing the same delicate chain around her chubby neck and I was indeed pleased.

Agnes had disclosed to me, that her son was soon to move away to Oxford, he had worked for the same, well to do employer, since his sixteenth birthday and had been offered promotion to work as their live-in head houseman. The offer had been made on the firm condition that he would travel with them; I saw that it made Agnes sad and I felt a great empathy for her.

I would make it my business, to ensure, that dear Agnes would have the means to visit her beloved son as often as possible. There would be a most deserving reward befitting such a hard working, gentle soul.

On returning to my room, I selected some bonds from Arthur's cabinet and signed the papers to my cook. Whatever was to become of me was irrelevant, as I cared not. However, the welfare of the kindly and honest woman, who had served me so faithfully, was of great importance and I would duly see to it that she was of sound fortune. I pressed on the stamp holding the family crest as it melted into the hot wax, to seal the letter.

Chapter 15

Mary

Chapter 15

Mary.

Continue with your search, Sargeant, for I will be long gone. My impostor continues with his fanciful falsehood, the game he plays without conscience. The letters will keep the police busy, of that, there is no doubt. It is fair that I do not wish to attract the unwanted attention and the truth will elude detectives for all time. Go back to hell Jack and take your letters with you! I have no need of your interference.

I discarded the evening newspaper, as I had no desire to read more nonsense about a man called Jack. I feared him not and I had no cause to worry. I would tread the dark streets in my crusade and Jack would take the blame.

Mary Kelly pulled her shabby and threadbare, woollen shawl, as tightly around her shoulders as she could. It was a very cold and misty November night and she was on one of her desperate quests, to locate some willing customers to sell her body to. All she required was a quick shilling or two, so that she had money to rest her head in a proper bed at the lodging house. Mary had already spent a few nights at the mercy of the cruel Whitechapel streets and another would do her in, for sure.

The streetwalker plied her trade the whole length of the square, but, there seemed to be no interest in the offerings between her legs. Mary had once lived the high-life; she had travelled most considerably and enjoyed high society status. What tragedy had befallen her, to succumb to such a life so distasteful and low, will always remain a mystery; however, Mary had become a wanton and desolate lady of the night; learning to live on her wits, trapped in her shameful futility. She was a troubled and ill-fated individual, an enigma, fallen so far from grace, that there was no return to the life she once had.

I observed her, as she walked the streets until her feet bled but I felt no sorrow for her plight, as this humble and fragmented soul that craved just a little affection. I felt only the pain of my own deep sorrow. The night was becoming colder by the minute and my patience began to err. I could not approach the lady whilst she remained in the glow of the street lamp, as I did not dare reveal myself.

I made my way across the road, I walked near to Mary and the stench of her made me wince. What madness is this, a wash, or a splash of lavender would surely bring forth a more favourable opportunity. I walked the other way, and passed by her again, she was obviously very beautiful, once, but life on the streets had robbed the allure from her face. The bewitching but filthy and unwashed whore, caught my gaze and she smiled sweetly, for a fleeting moment, before running along the cobbles to the far corner of Dorset Street.

A rather distinguished looking gentleman picked her up in his arms and smelled her all over. The random delights of man, how strange an individual pleasure can be! I recognised the man. I had noticed him at several of the parties we had attended in Westminster. I had taken tea with his wife and Arthur had played cards with him.

Who would have thought it possible, that the geographical restrictions would allow a man so charming and highly regarded, to wander so far from his place of residence, for the purpose of depravity. He was, on the surface, a most respectable and normal individual but in reality was discovered to be unfaithful and perverse.

I couldn't help but watch the purposeful degradation, despite it making me sick to my stomach. A wild animal released, on a woman so desperate. The debauchery was both lengthy and brutal and afterwards the man gave her some fruit and a handful of coins.

The man patted himself down and tipped his hat to the delighted Mary, then went on his way through Millers Court. Mary did a little dance and walked across the street. The dawn was already starting to break and I was aware that I had to readily avoid detection. I was constantly in fear of losing the cloak of darkness, so instead of chancing my luck, I decided to follow the skipping and dancing whore to the lodging house. I remained out of sight until I saw her enter the little house on the corner of Millers Court.

Mary secured a room, number 13, it was on the ground floor, it was small and had a bed and a small square table; there was a broken pane of glass that gave me a good view as she undressed and put herself to bed. She lay on her back and placed her arms above her head and I prayed that she would remain in that position as it would aid me greatly in my work.

When I was sure she was asleep, I put my hand through the broken window and set upon opening the latch. I climbed inside, unseen like a phantom. There were bottles and cartons on the table and I was careful not to disturb them, as I feared the noise would wake Mary up.

I stood over her and stared at the face that had lured our gentlemen to an odious and deadly affliction. I coveted her soft white breasts as I unbuttoned her under-bodice to gain access to her white torso. Despite the strange odour emanating from her, she had an eye for fashion and although her clothes were tattered and old, she carried in them an air of elegance. It was clear that she had not always suffered by poor fortune.

I dug my knife deep into the pulsing throat of Mary Kelly. Her life's blood sprayed the wall. She moved not at all, as I forced the knife around her breasts. I had not intended to remove them completely but once I had started there was no cause to stop, I also sliced at her arms and the flesh popped out, showing the whitish yellow of her bones, as the cuts zigged and zagged around her underarms and down to her fingers.

I worked silently, methodically and without fear of detection. I stopped for just an instant and peered out through the broken window, the street was still and quiet. I sat on the wooden chair and contemplated my work. Mary had a small mole on her groin and I flicked it off with the tip of my knife. I worked slowly and deliberately, as I had ample time to make my mark. I rested for a short while and sipped some water from one of the bottles on the table,

I was in the throes of euphoria, it was my finest act and it was perfectly executed.

Mary was intended to be my final project and I relished in the ability to finish the job properly. I slowly drew the knife from her groin to her neck and made deep cuts in her abdomen. I tried not to rush, it was hard not to, as during my previous tasks, I had been denied the privilege of time and light. It was a luxury to be afforded such a leisurely gratification and I delighted in it.

Blood soaked into the bed linen and it had a look of silk about it that pleased me. The chair at the side of the bed was handy, as I placed my tools on it. I chose carefully the implements for working on her face, as it is hard to break the bones inside a skull, and when the knife hits bone, it sometimes springs back into your hand and can cut you. I savoured the opportunity to choose my trophies with light to hand, it had been a struggle with the others, as although the dark was my cloak, it could also be a great hindrance and the visibility I was enjoying had a great effect on my aptitude.

I worked the knife inside Mary's stomach and removed my first trophy. I held her heart in my hands and watched the fresh blood as it slowly dripped to the floor. I placed it in the kettle, to wash it, the open valves, all shiny and grey, emptied as it flopped into the water and I anticipated the immense pleasure I would derive from watching it burn later. I carefully cut out her kidneys and placed them at her side. A little bubble appeared in the blood around her neck and I chopped at the flesh in the centre of her throat, just to check if there were a few more, as the popping sound was interesting. The usual adrenaline rush was far more intense, on this occasion and I was obliged to sit for a short while until it had passed.

The flesh on her thighs was warm still and it was like a balloon splitting as I cut the inner sides of them, the glossy, deep pink, muscles, tumbled freely onto the bed and I pulled them from the bones of her legs by the fibrous ligaments, before flaying open her calves. The caps in her knees were white as snow and I bent her legs to her stomach to watch them, as they popped effortlessly from the joints. Blood pooled on the wooden floor as it soaked through the mattress of the bed but it hindered me little.

I spent several hours cutting away the flesh from Mary's bones, it was a job well done, I broke her jaw and cut away the big tendons that moved it and then I sliced her tongue from her mouth. The bed-linen became increasingly wet from the bodily liquids that escaped each time a cut was made and the strain of the work made me sweat profusely. I picked up Mary's skirt and wiped my knife on it before placing it back on the neat pile on the floor. It had been a good idea to wait for her to undress herself, before I approached her, as it had saved me the trouble.

The room was sparsely furnished and it was helpful, as there were no obstacles in the way. Although the space was fairly small, the bed was pleasingly accessible and the table and chairs gave me a place to rest my tools and my being as I worked towards reaching my bloody climax.

I began to feel appeased, as Mary was the final name on the list hidden in Arthur's study. The list, I found, separated from the normal files, I did not fully understand the reason for this; my husband should not be in possession of such a list, there was no plausible explanation for it. I had always accompanied him on his numerous visits to the lost women. However, I had not assisted with the abortions of any of the women named.

I tried hard not to let the discovery shake my faith in my darling Arthur, it was not his fault; it was the fault of the demons inside the hearts and souls of the harlots he visited, that had tempted him. It had been beyond him, he was no match for the followers of Satan and they had managed to beguile him. I was certain of it, I was sure Satan had taken a hold on my darling, husband, Arthur, and it was not his fault. My husband was irrefutably innocent.

I concluded that Arthur must surely have found himself in the hopeless situation, where he had lost all control of his senses; caught up in the grip of lustful madness, an affliction that presented a hold on his soul and a pact with the devil.

I stood back and contemplated my work on Mary. She was still recognisable and I had the notion to remove all features from her, so that she became unreal and void of recognition as a human. I removed her eye and put it into my leather pouch with her kidney and I cut off both her ears. I forced the doctor's hammer inside her mouth and slammed my foot on it until I heard a loud crack. I then took the hammer from her shattered jaw and smashed it hard into the bridge of her nose. I hammered at her face until my arms fell down to my sides with exhaustion and I sat, again, on the simple wooden chair at her bedside and took another sip of water.

I found her liver and threw it between her feet, I cut out her intestines and scattered them around her and I put her left breast underneath her foot, so that I could slice into the bones below her ankle without having to lift her leg. I threw her spleen at her side and I shoved her other breast and her womb underneath her head like a little pillow, the stench of it all was nauseating but, it was a job well done.

It would serve as a good lesson, for those who abused their inner female wiles, to the detriment of all gentlemen. I suddenly experienced another familiar and powerful rush as I packed away my tools. An acute rush of elation the customary feeling; that completely overwhelmed my entire being, following each mission, it was a sense of triumph and fulfillment.

I sat awhile on the hard wooden chair, it was soiled with the blood of Mary, I still had a piece of her abdomen in my hand and I threw it on to the floor. At last, I was finally done. I carefully took and placed one of Mary's lifeless hands, deep inside her hollow torso and it seemed to give her the appearance of an empty soul searching for her lost womanhood.

Mary lay face upwards; she was sprawled on the blood-soaked bed, an empty vessel that was bereft of all life, soulless and too far gone to proclaim her innocence. Do not pray for Mary and the harlots of the streets. Pray instead for my lost husband and my babies, robbed of their lives.

I gathered my tools, closed the door and turned the small lock until it clicked, then I pushed the key underneath the front door before slipping out of sight into the grey mist of the morning. A little puzzle to tax your intelligence, Sargeant, as the key will surely give the illusion that the door has been locked from the inside.

Perhaps Jack will furnish you with another letter about it, but I think not, his letters will tell of things he knows nothing of, as he is furtive with his lies and he seeks attention in the foulest manner.

Written on parchment, or scrawled on a wall by the hand of a confused illiterate, a fabricator of the truth, a simple storyteller. An impostor, Sir, one who has no conception of the texture of pulled out organs or the smell of a fresh kill. The fate of the ragged women in the cobbled streets will not be atoned, I say to you, Sargeant, take no heed of he who goes by the name of Jack the Ripper, be now dismissive of his words and fanciful expressions, as despite your sound and extensive searching; the trials of my work will remain unsolved, as I am gone. Tonight I will slip into the shadows for the final time.

As I strolled through the misty greyness, past the square and the high arch into the yard, I remembered that I had forgotten to bring the heart from the pot. There would be no prized trophy to burn, no singed flesh transforming into hard black lumps, nothing to burn in the hearth, except the trivial bits and bobs I had snipped. The heart was one more small disappointment to contend with and I thought I had done so well. No matter, the mission had been a success, in as much as there were fewer atrocious whores to be contaminating our finest gentlemen. The ones that were left would be cautious and seek their money in other ways. The fear of Jack would see to that! The fear of a sinister man in a dark cloak would keep the cobbles clear.

An immense fatigue overwhelmed me as I reached the servants entrance and I could hardly climb the stairs. I had not eaten for days and my stamina had been depleted in the effort required during the recent atonement. I did not worry to bathe myself, as the servants would not return until the following evening and by that time I was sure to be revived. I climbed into my bed and hugged the pillow with Arthurs scent.

The ladies of the night were often subjected to physical attacks and it was not deemed unusual for a scream or a shout to be heard in the midst of the revelling. A black eye, or a bruise or two was a normal occurrence, as money-lenders and pimps sought easy cash by way of demand and forcefulness. Many atrocious attacks remained unreported, as the assaults were so commonplace that they held very little significance.

My cause, however, differed greatly, as it was my own way of saving mankind from vile and terminal diseases; it was personal, my private quest and an arbitrary release.

I had found a perfect cover for my simple acts, the fog and the dark were a natural curtain in my pursuance of revenge. The task had been swift and soundless, except for the subdued gurgle of life's oxygen as it escaped through the slit of a throat.

The journey home had been tedious, blood lay heavily on my clothes and the rank smell from bodily fluids had begun to rise up and offend me. My arms were tired; I had not envisaged the weight of internal organs and the effort of circumnavigating them had exhausted me. The blood had congealed to my clothes and they had become stiff and hard like a board.

My room was eerily quiet as the dawn cast a shadow across the wide floorboards; I undressed quickly and sponged the filth from my skin, then shoved the bloodied and filthy garments into the big sack from the box underneath the bed. I felt a warm glow of contentment envelop me as I fell into a dreamless sleep.

Chapter 16

Widow

Chapter 16

Widow

I sat at the window and stared wistfully into the garden below, I held my head in my hands as I tried to make sense of it all. I had become a widow at the age of just twenty four, bereaved of my darling, kind husband and of my stillborn twin boys; I glanced at my reflection in the huge ornate mirror above the dresser. The glass, shiny and bright, glinted in the afternoon sun. I was not at all charmed by it, as I longed for the night to fall.

I turned in my chair and stared at the huge wooden bed I once shared with my darling Arthur. The same bed he had died in. My beloved husband, what would become of me without him, he was gone, the subject of a cruel death full of pain and anguish. I clutched my torso in silent agony and I put my hand to my mouth to stifle my scream.

I tried my best to fight my inner fear but it was beyond my ability and I was lost in a profound despondency.

I missed my dear Arthur's gentle touch, I missed the smell of him and I missed his body next to mine in the big wooden bed. I threw myself onto the soft mattress and ached for a life denied to me.

The days ahead weighed too heavily for me, I was alone and my family was gone. I had been left with a legacy of only pain and loneliness and my heart burned with an agony I had never before witnessed. I languished in my private misery; I had no need of any comfort from others, as they could not possibly understand my pain. I wished for no soft words of encouragement, or scolding tongues urging me to be strong.

My tears would not fall and for what seemed like hours, I tossed and turned in my pain, until I slipped into an exhaustion induced sleep. I woke in the cold morning air and a wave of deep fear enveloped me. I managed to drag myself from the soft comfort of my bed and prepared a warm bath. I called for the maid to bring me some hot cocoa, I sipped the comforting fluid then I climbed into the tepid bathwater. I lay in the warmth, in the hope that my body would soon succumb; it would yield, I craved to be delivered to the same fate as my darling husband and my unborn infants. I had no idea what to do next and as I lay in the softness of the soapy water, I forged my greatest plan. Yes, I would redeem my beloved husband and in doing so, I would restore faith in myself and our good name and afterwards I would be free to join my family.

It made perfect sense to me and whoever would miss the stinking alley-cats, none, I say, except the ones that could spare a sixpence for a fumble in the dark. I seethed as I considered dutiful wives, hardworking and keeping good their family name, as their husbands made a mockery of their commitment and faithfulness.

Night time, was perfect for me, it would become the time that brought forth my anonymity, a time I could execute my task and a time I could extract my revenge. I would seek them out and carve them up then leave them on display. There would be no one to ever suspect me, I would go quietly about my business, in my own way and would slice them up to search for their souls and then I would send them to hell.

I would simply be stopping their breath from polluting the air; it would be my way of saving unsuspecting gentlemen from vile diseases, like the one that had killed Arthur. The pitiful sight of an intelligent and upstanding man as he fought for his life, on a bed soiled with his embarrassment, his final moments becoming racked with immense pain and insane ramblings, a cruel goodbye and a sickening legacy.

I would not allow, by any conscience, the ugly memories to leave me. I required the vision to remain with me, as it would help me focus and I quietly paid a visit to the servant's quarters to borrow a simple, neat grey cotton dress and a pinafore. I took an old shawl from the back of my closet and pulled it around my shoulders, then, I donned a dark straw bonnet, before creeping out into the night.

I was not sure which way to go at first, as I had not ventured outside in the darkness, without the company of my husband. So I walked aimlessly for about ten minutes, until I noticed a fine young gentleman as he hastily crossed the street towards one of the streetwalkers.

He glanced around cautiously and I could see the bulge in his breeches. He seemed slightly conscious of it and he put his hands down the front of them to rearrange himself. There appeared to be dozens of scantily clad ladies in the dim light of the gas lanterns, they made crude suggestions and lifted their skirts to show their legs.

They showed no shame as they worked the cobbled pavements, sashaying in their tardiness, as they emerged from the deep shadows to the lure of a few shillings. The hasty young man had disappeared into the dim light, where the whore stood with her arms behind her head as she arched her back and thrust her hips towards his groin.

She had no desire to know his name; he was her means to a bed for the night and a hot meal. His personality appeared to be of little concern; there was no requirement for a connection. A simple business transaction was taking place, as a quick and easy shilling could be made in the dim light of an alley.

I cast my eyes around the cold dark street and a wave of pity engulfed me, I put it out of my thoughts; I knew I had to have great strength and resilience, otherwise I would be unable to do what was required of me and my mission would surely fail, were I to create an empathy for the brazen, vile creatures of the streets.

The women of the night, the ones that had caused my unbearable anguish, the vulgar painted ladies with their ruffled petticoats and their grubby drawers, moist from the raw lust of their lewd customers.

I stood, invisible in the shadows; everyone around me was oblivious to my existence. I had the perfect disguise and I blended into the environment beautifully. I took note of the lamp-lighters, the Bobbies on the beat, the drunken men and the passers by. I watched them as they milled around the cobbles in their usual nightly manner I peeked through the windows of the many bustling taverns and inns and I saw beaten wives cry out for the husbands who drank away the rent. I considered all around me, but, for the most part I watched carefully the whores.

Chapter 17

Sargeant

Chapter 17

Sargeant

A kidney, a kidney in a letter, check you fools, for it is not from a human, perhaps a kidney from a pig. Jack, your letters tell of such untruths. Written, not in blood, I say but in red ink such as you can purchase in a bottle. Give grace and refrain from your lies. It is not a game, it is my mission and you have no idea of it.

The newspapers say that Jack the Ripper, is terrorizing the streets around the area of Whitechapel. Who is this individual, who calls himself Jack? Such a vagabond, and he, Jack the corrupt twister of the truth.

A leather apron a shoddy and vague clue from a discarded piece of cloth. The letter to the editor is not a clue that is made of accuracy but of a design to gain accolade. The casual mention of the Jews and the Polish immigrants, so many arbitrary and pointless clues, fear invoked falsehoods, that will accidentally incite hatred, bigotry and undue fear. Such a dishonest and time wasting, manner of deception such as will confuse those that assume to believe in sound integrity. The sordid letters in your hand, Sargeant, those words, so bold in red ink and filled with self indulgent and tiresome woes. Lies offered from the hand of the man with tainted vanity. Behold the frivolous arrogance possessed by such a hapless and befuddled man.

What other clues are required in order to test your resolve, I wrote a letter to you and your constables, but, I burned it, just like I burned the heart, the liver and the spleen. My confession eludes you, Sir, all traces are destroyed. No inkling, no easy means of detection, and my identity, dear Sir, will accompany me to my grave. Not too long now until my work is completed. Have no faith, Sir, as my wits are ten times that of yours.

Reality is compounded by ones grief and no intent to devalue mine will be tolerated as I am of sound mind and I bear one true crime, that which is only of a lost soul. I will not be one of your corrupt vagabonds, as I am not to be your jester.

Do not underestimate me and do not fear me, as I work only to redeem my husband. A good day's work will not find me, I am a shadow of the night. I refuse to hinder you, Sir. However, I will not offer you a false testimony. Take heed that your fair answers will never come, I am not about to reveal myself, for I am done with this world and no recognition for my crimes can stain me, as I offer myself to the devil himself.

That policeman of yours, the tall one, the Bobby on the beat, I know not his name only that I had stood by him and watched the confusion in his face as he struggled to make sense of his work. Good observation is the key, is it not? I was at his side and he knew me not!

A young servant girl, with a dirty face, to be dismissed from the scene, by his hand alone, for fear that the sight of it would perturb me. Scolding and loud with his concern, he took to hurrying me along. To make my haste away from the gathering crowd of onlookers, to be most fearful, as Jack was about.

A bewildered man, in search of a shadow and unaware that his floundering wretchedness, was my entertainment alone. I slid into the dimness and watched as the beat Bobby stood helpless in the midst of an angry mob.

The townsfolk were alarmed, they had consigned their fear and their fury to their neighbours; there was no one beyond their suspicion and they wanted safety returned to their streets. The air was rife with false testimony and the greatest excitement lead to careless accusations.

The gathering crowd will be a hindrance, as hundreds of men on the streets answer to the vague description of a wanted man and the chaos itself, will be causing a great wave of hysteria. The town will be in a state of unrest and I will watch from the shadows.

Make most careful investigations, Sir, if you will, as you are gaining no ground. Bring back your best detectives to hunt me down, as perhaps those with a local knowledge of these teeming slums will be required to survey the veritable labyrinths of dirty streets, where the narrow, unlit alleyways and passages enable me to do my work, then melt into anonymity.

None will yield my identity and the list of suspects will continue to grow. Do not seek out our simple butchers, or barbers or those who work in the slaughter houses, for they are innocent. Take no pleasure in the accusations towards the immigrants as they are not guilty, they are just different. The leather apron is that which was lost by reasonable means and is not up for question. Distrust, is a word that will be used heavily and something that will soon abound between your inspectors and the journalists; Take little heed of those whom without the appropriate and fair authority; will seek to dispense most alarming and sensational advice to their avid audience.

Dismiss your preconceived ideas, for my fate is a foregone conclusion. There are no answers, Sargeant and your questions are futile and give insult to my cause.

Chapter 18

Valet

Chapter 18

Valet

I mused a little before putting pen to paper for my dismissal letter to Samuel, I had failed miserably to take a fair liking to my husband's valet and I had no trust in him; it was simply a feeling but I had always valued my instinct and he did not sit well with me.

In total contrast, my dear Arthur had been extremely fond of Samuel and had trusted him implicitly. Not I, for I was sure that he most certainly had knowledge of my husband's misdeeds, where did he wait as he escorted him to Whitechapel, in order to visit the ladies of the night. Did he so witness his unfaithful master, did he hold his cloak and his gloves as he caressed the thighs and breasts of the harlots, his breath hot on their pulsing necks, as they ground their private parts in unison.

My husband held his aide in the highest esteem, I had no stomach for him, I placed my quill in the inkwell and rose from my chair, I had no charitable words to put to paper, Samuel had been servant to Arthur, not me and I found his presence abhorrent.

I paced the floor and my head pounded in a vain search for something to write, but the words failed me so I put the unmarked parchment aside and called for Polly to bring me some tea.

A hot cup of tea is a surprising aid to any blurred notion and it would do me well on this occasion to calm myself. I knew that Arthur would be very disappointed with my decision to fire Samuel and I struggled with the vexation of it.

Samuel had enjoyed a good wage, well above average for his post and the very generous amount of fifty five pounds, he received each year was ten pounds more than most others in the same role. Arthur had insisted that he was indeed worth it and would offer no less. I had agreed on the premise that Agnes and Polly were to be given appropriate consideration and ours were the highest paid domestic staff in the whole of London town.

I sat at my writing desk and this time the words flowed effortlessly. I bequeathed to Samuel, all Arthurs clothes, his collection of cigars, the leather case with the lock, the one he used to transport his papers in: I proposed the gold cufflinks and the cases of wine from the cellar.

The horses and the carriage with the gold trim on the wheels, I gave, not really for benefit to Samuel but because I knew he loved Shadow and Midnight and would look after them properly. I counted two hundred pounds from the safe that was hidden behind the painting of my parents; the one that hung in the drawing room, the one that was my most favourite of all. I stared wistfully at the oily canvas, as I placed the cash in a large brown packet and sealed it with the mark of Arthur.

There, Samuel, a good job has been done, take this fair payment for your service to a man no longer your master and be gone from this place.

I served no reference to a future employer but Samuel had been rewarded enough.

Chapter 19

Memories

Chapter 19

Memories

The end of 1888 was upon us, it was time, I wonder if they discovered the heart of Mary Kelly, hidden in the big copper pot. I wonder how long Jack would continue with his letters, so elusive and dishonest. I wonder what they will deduce when my work is no more and I wonder if they will find my small clue.

A cold day ensued on Sunday the 31st of December 1888; the house was empty and quiet. I had given the servants the entire weekend off. Agnes had gone to visit her son and Polly had taken Jim home to meet her parents. I had a feeling there would be a proposal very soon and I was happy for my sweet young maid.

I had no idea where Samuel had gone, I assumed he was with friends at the other end of town but I cared not. I had plenty of time to prepare myself and was grateful for the uninterrupted privacy. I climbed the stairs to the attic and sifted through the big trunk that contained my memories. I took the photographs of our wedding day and spread them over the floor, it should have been our anniversary, I should have been happy, a darling husband and two precious children, but, instead of this, I was condemned to a long, lonely solitude. It was a fate I had never envisaged. It was one year to the day my husband had died and a week before my 25th birthday.

I studied the photographs for a while, then I read Arthurs letters, so full of love and consideration for our life together. I read the poems he sent me from his trips away and I put his wedding ring in my mouth. I removed my own ring and thread it on the fine chain around my neck.

I went downstairs and made myself some cocoa then tidied up the kitchen. I drew a bath and stepped into the soothing water. I wanted to shed some tears but they simply would not flow.

My pain engulfed me and I felt as void of life, as the women I had recently killed.

I hugged my torso in absolute grief, for my lost babies and a pain so intense, that it caused me to cry out, seared through me as I swallowed Arthur's gold band. I had no remedy for my broken heart and I welcomed the release soon to come.

I took a final walk around our beautiful house, a home for our lost family, now an empty box with no souls to fill it. I opened the doors and peered into each room, I felt the urge to close the shutters but I had no idea how to secure them. The grandfather clock in the hallway struck two and my heart sank to the pit of my stomach.

I took the soiled garments from underneath the bed and shoved them into an old carpet bag that once belonged to Arthur: I would throw it into one of the many street braziers as I passed on my way. I left the wrap of tools in the box. A little clue that none but I, or Jack could decipher.

I collected the four sealed letters from the desk in the drawing room and placed them in the pocket of my gown, then I climbed the stairs, stopping only to touch the oily face on the portrait of Arthur that hung so boldly outside our bedroom door. The most perfect masterpiece, of a once loved master who was no more: The weight of my grief consumed me as I began to make ready for my new journey,

Chapter 20

Goodbye

Chapter 20

Goodbye

The house was peaceful and it smelled, still, of lavender from the bath. I lay naked on the bed, desolate in my quiet solitude; the monotonous tick of the clock was my only company and I had no desire for any more.

I pulled on my undergarments and hitched my stockings to my garter. I brushed my hair and drew it neatly back into the tight chignon that Arthur found so appealing. I took out the gown I had placed at the front of my closet; it was the one I wore on my wedding day. The one Arthur had said I looked perfect in. I carefully draped the dress over the bottom of the wooden bed and studied the elegance of the fabric. The garment was very beautiful, it was made of dark blue taffeta with a layered sky blue and ivory bustle, the high necked bodice had tiny pink pearls sewn into the lace and the skirt had swags of pale blue and ivory satin. I wanted to look my very best for my important journey, and for

Arthur and my babies. I located my brown satin booties and the delicate hat with the pink and blue feathers on it. It all matched perfectly and I knew I had chosen well.

I lay across the bed for a short while; the pillows were plump and soft, one of them still had traces of Arthur's cologne, it had lingered despite being washed and I filled my nostrils with the scent, for one last time. I finally got up and pulled on my blue dress, then slipped my feet into the soft boots. I stood before the full length mirror and studied my reflection. It was reminiscent of the day I went to meet my husband, at the little church in Islington and this evening I would go to meet him again

I heard the clock chime, four and I donned my velvet coat with the hood and the large pockets at the sides, before taking a deep breath in order to compose my soul, in my readiness to venture outside.

I took a final walk around the house; I chose two apples from the big china bowl in the kitchen and popped them into my pocket as a last treat for the horses. The stables were deserted. I spent a quiet minute with dear Midnight and Shadow; they snorted and chomped at the ripe fruit they enjoyed so much, and I held their damp nostrils and patted their soft flanks before kissing their beautiful faces, The horses were proud and elegant, I had so loved the rides and the sound of their hooves clip clopping, as they pulled the carriage along the uneven cobbled streets,.

It was ten minutes past four, so I still had a full twenty minutes, to reach the bridge at my chosen time of four-thirty; it would take me approximately ten minutes or so on foot, which left me just ten minutes to place the letters in the servants quarters, and to check that everything was left as I desired.

Polly's room was neat and tidy, her clean pinafore hung on a hook by the door and her flannel dress and shawl were folded in a little pile, on the chair by her bed; she had very few personal possessions and it made me sad, that I had not noticed until now. I placed the letter containing her fair reference, the five bonds worth a hundred pounds each and fifty, crisp, one pound notes; on her dresser. I had bequeathed her two of my favourite gold necklaces, my diamond tiara and the solid silver from the cabinet in the grand hallway. It would be a fortune to someone like her and would set her up nicely for her new life with Jim.

I crossed the landing to the pretty room that had been the home of Agnes for so many years. I sat at the edge of her neatly made feather bed: It pleased me that I had been able to provide such comfort for my faithful staff and I knew that our respect was mutual. I stood the letter to my dear cook, up against her mirror. The contents were similar to that of Polly; however, the bonds were worth a hundred pounds more.

I carefully placed my fine ebony jewellery box, containing a little note, on the table at the window; it gave the details of a fair pawnbroker, who was bound to give her good value. I requested a small favour in return and I felt assured that it would be granted, as I had known Agnes for a very long time. For a fleeting moment, I felt an overwhelming surge of deep affection, for Agnes and for Polly and it was all I could do not to weep, as I quickly descended the stair-well and hurried across the landing towards the room occupied by Samuel.

The letter I had left in the careful charge of Agnes was for our family solicitor, he was to sell the house and the contents; the proceeds of which were to be placed in a charitable trust for the poor unfortunates of Whitechapel. A strange request, I have to concede, however, as I had wandered the cobbles at night, I had come to realise, that many of the residents may require sound assistance, rather than contempt.

Perhaps not the vile slums, infested with heathens and grubby, flame haired strumpets, I had first perceived; perhaps more a society to be rescued. Alas, it really made no difference, to me, as I was indeed done with it. A simple cook, with a fortune to hand, would be the one to save them and bring honour to the lives of the dammed.

I took the letter for Samuel and left it on the table by his dresser. It was the very first time I had set foot inside his private quarters. He appeared to own many, rather expensive items and there was a pouch of farthings open, with the contents scattered on his writing desk. His room was elegant and large and I was convinced that it was payment for secrets.

I made my way downstairs and stood for a moment in the vast hallway. I resented the almost shameful and wasted extravagance. The meaningless opulence was now of no relevance, as my desires were no longer for inanimate trinkets, I placed the letter for Charlotte by the carriage clock on the mantel, I presumed she would find it in the morning, when she came to lead the hearth. I glanced around in distain, I did not look behind me, as I walked towards the threshold of my marital home and I closed the door for the very last time.

I strolled through the wide avenues, past the large, elegant gated homes, that failed to conceal the wealth of those who owned them. I skirted the park, choosing to walk the long way towards my final destination and I took advantage of my damask fan to shield my face from any person that might recognize it. The December breeze was a little icy and I pulled my hood closer, as I stepped purposefully along the frost covered pavements.

Colourful and immaculately kept terraced houses swept along the wide avenues that led to the river. It was a far cry from the putrid stench of the cobbled streets, where grainy washing hung across the narrow alleyways and roads. A pit, of flea ridden and hapless, individuals, existing day to day, on the cobbled streets, in a Godless place, where dirty carts and underfed horses left mess in their wake and children played in their grubby oblivion.

A tragic place, deep in the slums of the East End, grey and unforgiving of a life, set in the airless quarters and the humble lodgings, where many a shadowy figure lurked in the misty darkness.

A tale would emerge of a titled lady, who bequeathed her fortune, in her endeavours to compound the appalling conditions of the unfortunates, hopelessly compelled to endure their lot. All temptation to attribute the credit to me would be quashed, as I had arranged for all my wealth to be distributed without my name to the written, legal documents. I had taken great pride in the humility of surreptitiously making my amends and the cost had been diminutive.

For the police and the newspapers will never know the truth, the answers will not come; they will remain with me even after I have drawn my last breath. Put vague and futile thoughts of Jack the Ripper, out of question, as who knows, perhaps it was Jane!

I climbed to the side of the tower; I stared into the murky water far below me. Thank you Jack, for your helpful camouflage, I wish you well, on your self-indulgent and attention seeking quest for your moment of fame. You have no concept of how it feels to take a life, how it feels to hold the tools of murder in your hands, or the rush of adrenaline as a life ebbs from a spent soul. Good luck, Jack the Ripper. I fear you not, for I know you not and you are not real, you are but an impostor, with a pen to hand; a quill of blood red ink and lies. Be gone, with your cavalier attitude and idle mischief, your stained postcards a fools pleasure; a news editor's inspiration, and a source of titillation for the readers.

The wind was very cold around me and I shivered as I reached down to feel inside the large pockets of my coat, for the heavy stones I had gathered from the riverbank.

My work was done on this earth; a time for rest was upon me. I had suffered more than I deserved and I had caused pain and suffering to others. I was sick of the world and its ugliness. How I had come to this place was but a blur in my irrational mind.

The demise of the wretched whores from the cobbles meant not a thing to me and I had no remorse, however, I had to admit, that, for a passing moment, my agonized heart cried out for the anguish it would cause their loved ones, those left behind. I hoisted myself up to the top and teetered on the narrow, ornate side ledges of the high bridge, I would be chastised for my self-murder, I was fully aware of that and my empty body would be dragged from the deep blackened water of the Thames. I feared it may even be unceremoniously paraded to the public; mercilessly dragged around, swollen with the fight for air, then buried face down at a crossway, so that my futile spirit would be confused and not know which way to go.

My family and that of Arthur would suffer also from the shame of my self-murder. They will say I went mad: They will say I could not live without my husband at my side. The newspapers will tell stories of a timid and weak woman, too frail to face a widow's fate, a young woman, lost to the lunacy of a tortured mind and society will forever scorn my memory.

They may put a wooden stake through my heart, to keep my suicidal demons from roaming the land. I know this, as it had been done to others that had dared to commit suicide. It was deemed that these things would serve as a fitting punishment for the sins against God.

But, how little I should care, for I would be with my dear husband and my darling babies! I would never deny them my love.

It was four thirty on December the 31st 1888, when I released my grip from the hard and cold metal that had held me safe, as I climbed the iron railings to the ornate ledge at the highest part of the old stone bridge. I felt nothing except a release from my living hell, as with a huge sigh of relief; I fell into the deep murky water of the Thames.

Fret no more, poor, sweet ladies of the night, as peace to you, I swear, and during the worrisome years that will follow my most covert and watery demise; fear not, for it will truly become apparent to all, that the murders will have ceased.

******

Copyright © Irene husk 2020

Perhaps it was Jane cover - by RDesigns

Perhaps it was Jane

By Irene Husk
2020

All rights reserved.   *R.R.P. £9.99*

Thank you to everyone who supported me as I wrote this book, especially my ever patient husband, Dean who gives me the quiet and space.

Horses names chosen by Emily.

It's not really that easy to live a positive life with negative thoughts, if you don't leave your past where it belongs, it will destroy your chances of a happy and successful future.

So live for what today has to offer and not for what yesterday has taken away.

No part of this book may be reproduced or used in any manner whatsoever without the prior written consent of the author.

It must not be loaned or borrowed

Nor may it be distributed or otherwise circulated in any form of cover or binding other than that in which it was originally published.

With thanks to my family and friends for all the support, encouragement and constructive criticism.

Author

Photograph by The Studio18, Potters Bar, Herts.

I pulled the folds of my shawl around me and slipped into the park. It was shrouded in darkness and the only sounds to be witnessed: were that of the lewd grunting customers, as they went about their loathsome gratification; the results of which could be so randomly cast away from the wombs of the desperate women.

I hurried along in my own private misery and crept through the ornate gates and into the house by the servant's entrance, unseen and unheard.

I climbed the wide stairs to the sanctity of my room. There, I hid the simple cotton dress and shawl in a big cloth sack, I put it in a box underneath my bed and I washed the stickiness from me.

****

Put vague and futile thoughts of Jack the Ripper out of question as who knows, perhaps it was Jane!

Although the said victims of Jack the Ripper were described as lower, or working class prostitutes, we can never forget that they were human beings, caught up in the failure of society to serve them well. They made their living the only way they knew how. Each life contains its own merit and the loss of a single soul is infinitely tragic. These unfortunate women had pretty faces that smiled, they had softness and kind hearts; they possessed personalities that set them apart as individuals. They enjoyed close families and friends and they suffered in their desperation. Dismiss them not simply as victims, as their lives were of worth to the people who loved them. Do not remember them as whores: Remember instead, the spirits of those who must be valued as much as any other fallen angel.

My Bite Size Books

Author

Irene Husk

Irene was born in the valleys of South Wales. She enjoys writing in an easy to pick up and put down style, using short chapters and a quick flow, in cross genre subjects.

Irene also writes as Sheila Cooper

Copyright 2020/hiPIWJ

Printed in Great Britain
by Amazon